"You've never had bad sex?" Charlie asked incredulously.

"No. No, I haven't," Mark said as they walked into the elevator. He sounded surprised that she'd even ask. "Why, have you?"

"Of *course.* I thought everyone had."

"Not me. How could you? I mean, everything about it is so wonderful. It doesn't matter if you're cramped, or the temperature's not right, or you don't have a lot of time. It's still..." Mark's eyes glowed as he gazed into hers. "Making love is great," he finished softly. "And this will be the best."

Charlie looked away from him. "Now I'm really intimidated. I could be your first disaster."

"No way. After all, women are designed for pleasure. How could you end up with anything else?" He took her hand and pulled her closer. "Hold on, let me show you what I mean."

As he brought his lips down to hers in a kiss that set her pulses racing, Charlie moaned her appreciation. Apparently she'd stumbled onto a man who was an artist when it came to making love, and tonight he planned to create a masterpiece.

Who was she to argue with that?

Dear Reader,

I'm a catalog shopper, so the MAIL ORDER MEN series makes perfect sense to me. It must make sense to you, too, because it's been so popular the first and second time out that we're offering a third batch of cuties, just in time for spring! So set aside your Neiman-Marcus catalog for a minute and imagine that a copy of *Texas Men* has just landed in your mailbox. Hey, who wants to look at clothes and shoes when you can admire the likes of Mark O'Grady, *Texas Men*'s Bachelor of the Month?

Watching bachelors become husbands is a favorite part of my job as romance writer, but this time the familiar story held special significance for me. As I recorded Mark's progress toward the altar, my son Nathan was making a similar journey. He married his dream girl, Lauri, shortly after I provided Mark with his happy ending. But for Nathan and Lauri, this is only the beginning of the story they will write together. And I wish them a lifetime of happiness...without end.

Best wishes from the mother of the groom,

Vicki Lewis Thompson

P.S. In June look for my novella "Mystery Lover" in *Midnight Fantasies*, the 2001 Blaze collection. And in August don't miss *Notorious*, one of the launch books in Harlequin's sizzling new series BLAZE.

Vicki Lewis Thompson
EVERY WOMAN'S FANTASY

HARLEQUIN®

TORONTO • NEW YORK • LONDON
AMSTERDAM • PARIS • SYDNEY • HAMBURG
STOCKHOLM • ATHENS • TOKYO • MILAN • MADRID
PRAGUE • WARSAW • BUDAPEST • AUCKLAND

For Nathan and Lauri—
Your courage and belief in each other inspires me.

ISBN 0-373-25926-3

EVERY WOMAN'S FANTASY

Copyright © 2001 by Vicki Lewis Thompson.

This edition published by arrangement with Harlequin Books S.A.

Visit us at www.eHarlequin.com

Printed in U.S.A.

_____Prologue_____

"I CAN'T BELIEVE you did it again."

Mark O'Grady glanced across the table littered with peanut shells and a couple of half-empty beer bottles. His very pissed-off best man Sam Cavanaugh, who'd uttered those words of disgust, sat across from him, still dressed in his tux. So was Mark. Going back to his apartment to change had seemed too risky.

Fortunately he and Sam were the only ones of their crowd who patronized this little bar in downtown Houston. Their friends considered it too shabby, which was fine with Sam and Mark, who had designated it their special hidey-hole ever since they'd been old enough to drink legally. And Mark needed a place to hide...again.

He tried to come up with something to say to Sam, but he couldn't think of a damned thing. He was slime. Somebody should just shoot him.

"Ten minutes before the processional! Ten friggin' _minutes._ How could you _do_ that?"

"It was her cell phone," Mark said.

"What do you mean, her _cell phone?_ I fail to see how anything about a cell phone could cause you to back out of your wedding ten minutes before the ceremony. If Deborah hadn't smashed her wedding bouquet in your face, I would have done it for her!"

Mark gazed at his long-suffering friend. "You're

right. It was horrible, and I should have figured it out sooner. We'd had some big arguments about how much she used that phone. She took it everywhere, and I mean *everywhere*, and it's not like the calls were critical or anything. Most of them sounded like a lot of gossip to me. But I kept thinking it was a small issue. I could deal."

"It *is* a small issue. The woman has friends. She likes to talk to them on the phone. If you love somebody, you put up with a few things that aren't perfect about them." Sam gave him another disgusted look before taking a swallow of his beer and setting it on the table with a clunk. "God knows you're a long way from being perfect."

"You've got that right." Mark turned his beer bottle around and around in his hands. "And I told myself all that. I thought I was fine with her cell phone habit. Then, remember how we were going up to the altar to take our places, and we passed by that room where Deb and her bridesmaids were waiting, and the door was open?"

"Yeah, I most certainly do. Because that's when you lost it and called the whole thing off."

"There she was, in her wedding dress, looking gorgeous, and she had that damned cell phone to her ear, jabbering away to somebody. I couldn't even imagine who she'd find to talk to! Every person she knew was sitting in the church!"

"That is kind of amazing, when you think about it," Sam conceded. "Maybe she was talking to somebody who was in the church, someone who also had their cell phone turned on."

"No doubt! And I don't want any part of that! I saw our whole married life dominated by that thing. The wedding night, the honeymoon, the delivery room when we had a kid, the family vacations, the visits to the folks. I mean, if she had to talk on the phone ten minutes before we were about to say our vows, then nothing was sacred."

Sam blew out a breath. "Okay, I can see your point. I wouldn't like that prospect myself, but I sure as hell wish you'd figured all this out sooner."

"So do I."

Leaning both arms on the table, Sam trained his no-nonsense look, the one he used to intimidate juries, on Mark. "In case you've lost count, this is the fifth time this has happened. None of your friends except yours truly will show up anymore. Even your mother refuses the invitations. Is it possible you don't want to get married?"

Mark had given that considerable thought himself. He'd been raised by a single mother who'd divorced his father when Mark was two. She'd never remarried, and when he was old enough to ask about that, she'd told him she found marriage too confining and time-consuming.

Because she was all he had, he'd tried to see things her way. But he couldn't help envying kids like Sam, who had a cozy family with two parents and a bunch of noisy siblings. Finally he'd decided he couldn't agree with his mother. Although the single life might suit her, he wanted to find a woman to share his life and be the mother of their kids.

He met Sam's gaze. "I do want to get married. It's divorce I want to avoid."

"At this rate you'll never have to worry about divorce, old buddy. Now if you'll excuse me, I'm going to the can. You can sort through your options while I'm gone."

Mark watched his friend leave. Sam appeared to be in no rush to get married, and yet the guy was extremely eligible. With his dark blond mustache and lean good looks, he was often mistaken for Alan Jackson. Plus he was a successful lawyer and drove a beautifully restored red '57 Chevy that always drew attention. Yet he'd only been engaged once, and that hadn't lasted more than two months before they'd both decided they weren't right for each other.

Obviously Sam wasn't desperate to create a family for himself because he'd had that growing up. Mark had hungered for that kind of stability ever since he could remember. But he wasn't any closer to getting it than he had been seven years ago, when he'd proposed to Hannah, his first fiancée. Something had to change, but he didn't know what.

The waitress came by and he ordered another round. Then he called her back. "Add a shooter to the beer," he said. "No, wait. *Five* shooters." It seemed like a fitting number.

The waitress blinked. "Five? All at once?"

"Yep." Mark held up his hand, fingers spread. "And you might as well bring five for my buddy, too." When the waitress continued to stare at him, he added, "We'll both be taking cabs home, so don't worry."

With a nod, the waitress left.

Mark decided if he couldn't figure out how to fix his sorry situation, he might as well get drunk with Sam. He could bail his Lexus out of the parking garage in the morning.

An extra few hours of parking expense was nothing compared to the bills he had run up with these five canceled weddings. In each case, he'd let his fiancées keep the rings and even go on the honeymoon if they could find somebody else to go along. Three had taken that option, and two had said they'd rather rot in hell. Deb had been one of those.

On top of that, Mark had covered the cost of the reception and other incidentals. He hadn't wanted his fiancées or their families to suffer financially, considering they'd be suffering emotionally. If he hadn't brokered his talent for playing the stock market into a lucrative career, he'd really be in the poorhouse. As it was, the weddings had eaten up any financial gains he'd made.

With that depressing thought, he started on the shooters the waitress had brought.

Sam took quite a while returning, and when he finally did, he eyed the shot glasses lined up on the table. "I take it the number is significant?"

Mark had already polished off three of his. "You betcha. Pull up a seat and get started. You're behind. What took you so long?"

"The waitress stopped me to ask if we were in here for the same reason as the last couple of times. I had to offer her ten bucks to keep her from coming over here and pouring a pitcher of beer on your head."

"Thanks." The shooters were starting to kick in, slowly taking the tension out of his body. Ah, this was much better.

Sam sat down and threw a magazine on the table. "I found some interesting reading material in the john," he said. "I think this might be the answer."

Mark tossed down the fourth shooter and picked up the magazine. *"Texas Men?"* He leafed through the ads for eligible bachelors, then glanced over at Sam and grinned. He was getting *very* relaxed, relaxed enough to find Sam's gesture hilarious. "Sorry to dis'ppoint you, but I'm stickin' with girls."

"You are so dense. No wonder you're such a mess. I'm suggesting we put *you* in that magazine."

"Why?" Mark was beginning to feel really goofy. "So I can rack up more broken engagements? Get in the *Guinness Book of World Records?*"

"No, the exact opposite. I'm trying to prevent another broken engagement. Here's what we'll—"

"Hey. I'll be a monk. Should've thought of that before. Where's the nearest monastery? I'll turn myself in." He picked up the last shooter. "Come on, Sammeeee. Get blitzed with me."

"Shut up and listen. I've thought about this, and the reason you get engaged to the wrong women is that they're beautiful, and so naturally you have sex with them."

"Nat-u-ral-ly." Mark spoke carefully so he wouldn't slur. "Sex's good."

"Except underneath that swinging bachelor exterior of yours, you have old-fashioned ideas. You think because you had sex, you should get married."

"True-de-doo-doo. And I'm grateful." He smiled at Sam. "Sooo grateful. Women are wunnerful, Sam. They smell so good, and they feel terrific, and…I love 'em, Sam. I want to marry one of them. I really, really do."

"You are stewed to the gills, aren't you?"

"Yep."

"Maybe that's just as well. You're more likely to agree to my plan if you're pickled. Here it is—we put an ad for you in this magazine, and then we sort through the prospects and find somebody perfectly suited to you. After that you write letters for a long time. A very, very long time. And during that correspondence, you find out if they're addicted to cell phones, or hate camping, or any of the other stupid reasons you've backed out."

"Not shtupid."

"Okay, they're not stupid. But with this woman, you're getting that all settled way in advance. Every possible glitch that would be a sticking point will be discussed, and analyzed, and dissected, *ad nauseum*."

Mark frowned. "Don't like writin' letters."

"I don't care. I don't frigging care!" Sam jabbed a finger at him. "This is tough-love time. You are going to write those letters, and you'll get to know this person before you meet her, before you even *think* of going to bed with her. Because I know you, and once you do the nasty, you'll propose. Do you understand what I'm saying?"

"Yeah." Mark nodded slowly, so the room wouldn't start spinning. "I'm gonna have a pen pal." He paused to think. "And I'm not gettin' any for a long, lo-o-o-ng time."

1

Six months later

"ASHLEY, I'M SCARED." Charlie McPherson watched her older sister close out the cash register for the day. Ashley had worked her butt off in retail for five years and now owned Glam Girl, home to some of Austin's trendiest fashions.

Ashley glanced up. "About what?"

"Mark wants to meet me." Charlie wasn't into fashion, which was why she desperately needed advice and moral support from her big sis.

"Hey, you'll be fine." Ashley smiled. "Perfectly fine. He's a lucky guy."

"You're my sister. You're supposed to say that."

Ashley gazed at her. "I don't blame you for being nervous," she said gently. "Let me finish up here and we'll go get a couple of big old margaritas and talk about it."

"That would be good." Margaritas would definitely help give her the courage to explain her problem.

If she looked more like Ashley, she might not be so scared. Her sister could just as well be modeling fashions as selling them. Charlie envied three things about Ashley. She was nearly five-eight, which allowed her to wear every outfit in the store without hemming it. Secondly, her rich brown hair was wavy, not curly like

Charlie's, so she could wear it long. Last of all, their parents had given Ashley a terrific name which required no fiddling to make it sound right.

Charlie had to hem up almost everything she bought, and if she didn't keep her blond hair short, she looked like Medusa. As for her name, she was still ticked off at her folks for saddling her with Charlene. Nobody these days was named Charlene.

She'd shortened it to Charlie, which sounded more twenty-first century and suited her outdoor lifestyle, but it wasn't half as distinctive as Ashley. Of course, Charlie had to admit she didn't *look* like an Ashley. Ashley belonged to someone elegant, like her sister. Nobody had ever accused Charlie of being elegant. Cute, bouncy, full of energy, yes. Never elegant. Making Charlie elegant would take a miracle.

Twenty minutes later, as Charlie sat across from Ashley at their favorite Tex-Mex restaurant, she was hoping her big sister would help her pull off that miracle.

"Here's to a great first date with Mark O'Grady." Ashley lifted her frosty glass and touched it to Charlie's.

"Amen." Charlie took a sip of her drink and set it on the square cocktail napkin. Then she looked over at her sister. "The thing is, when Mark suggested we write to each other for several weeks so we could really learn about each other before we met, I got this idea."

Ashley put down her drink, too. "Which was?"

"I decided to change my image."

She had Ashley's total concentration now. "To what?" she asked carefully.

"Well, you know how most guys treat me like the girl

next door. They see me as wholesome, low-maintenance, stuff like that."

"Charlie, that's because you are those things. They're all pluses, in my book."

"Whatever. The point is that in my whole life, I have never made a guy drool."

"Oh." Ashley gazed at her and the wheels were obviously going around. "So what kind of image does Mark have of you?"

"I didn't lie or anything," Charlie said quickly. "I mean, he knows I work for an outdoor adventure company, and he's seen my picture so he knows what I look like. But I made him think that underneath that girl-next-door persona I'm also this...well, this really hot babe. I, um, wrote some pretty racy stuff, things I probably would never have the nerve to say in person."

Ashley looked taken aback, but gradually her green eyes warmed. "Ah, I get it. You're afraid that when you two meet, he'll expect to jump into bed right away, and you're not ready for that."

"But I am ready for that."

Ashley blinked. "You are? Oh, Charlie, I don't think that's a very good idea. You need to—"

"I need to experience unbridled passion for once in my life! With every other guy I've dated, there's no mystery, no tension, no *lust*. But now I have that. We've had three months of postal foreplay. We are *so* loaded with tension. I just don't want to mess up and diffuse it."

Ashley stared at her. Then she took a quick drink of her margarita and cleared her throat. "Okay, let me get my bearings here. I can understand wanting to make a guy lust after you. But I can't go along with the hopping-into-bed part. I realize you've exchanged a lot of letters with Mark, but that's not the same as face-to-face contact. You need to give it more time before you get into a physical—"

Charlie let out a gusty sigh. "You sound so 'older sister.' Haven't you ever gone to bed with a guy on the first date?"

Ashley blushed. "We're not talking about me."

"What? We should live by different rules?"

Her sister looked disconcerted. "Well, I—"

"Exactly. We shouldn't. Now I'm not saying I *will* go to bed with him right away, but I might, if I don't mess it up and come on like a camp counselor on the first date. I want you to help me look like a sex goddess."

Ashley's eyes widened. "If Mom and Dad could hear this conversation, they'd have a hissy-fit. I'm supposed to look out for you, not help you get into trouble."

"Oh, so that's it. Look, when I moved to Austin I was twenty-two. Maybe I needed some looking after. But hel-*lo*, I'm five years older now! I'm even older than you were when I got here. And, damn it, I want to feel sexy and glamorous for once in my life. Will you help me or not?"

Ashley studied her for a long moment. "I don't know. This feels sort of weird. Do you have any idea where he'll take you on this first date?"

"Not yet."

"Well, once you know that, I'll...I'll at least help you find something great to wear."

"Great as in nice, or great as in hot?"

"Oh, God." Ashley looked at her and shook her head. "Unbridled lust? Are you sure that's what you want?"

"Yep."

Ashley rolled her eyes. "Mom and Dad would have a cow."

"CHARLIE'S PERFECT. My dream girl. My soul mate. My happily-ever-after." Mark brushed peanut shells from the table and wiped away a ring of moisture left by his empty beer bottle before laying a dog-eared picture on the table in front of Sam. "Look at that face and tell me she's not perfect."

"I've seen her face. In case you've forgotten, I'm the one who picked her out of the stack and told you she had promise."

"And you were right!"

"It remains to be seen whether I was right," Sam said. "All the information isn't in yet."

"Most of it. And her letters are so...friendly. I think she looks exactly the way her letters sound, don't you?"

Sam picked up the picture and studied it. Then he handed it back to Mark. "Okay, so she's a good prospect on paper, but with your record, I don't think you should rush into—"

"Sam, I'm ready to meet her. I'm *so* ready to meet her." He tucked Charlie's picture in his shirt pocket, right next to his heart.

Sam gave him the evil eye. "You said that with a little too much relish, good buddy. Just exactly what do you mean by *meet*?"

Mark threw up both hands. "I mean just meet! Like drive to Austin for the weekend, and—"

"Slow down, lover-boy! Are we talking an overnight here?"

"Well, yeah. If I take her out for a nice dinner somewhere, with wine, and candlelight, and…and stuff, then I don't want to drive all the way back to Houston that same night."

Sam leaned forward. "Dinner's fine, candlelight and wine is terrific. But it's the *and stuff* part that's got me worried. I'm coming with you."

"No way! Nobody's chaperoned my dates since I was fourteen, and I'm not about to reactivate the custom now."

Sam gazed at him for a long time, as if he was turning something over in his mind. Finally he settled back against the worn cushion of the booth with a sigh. "I hate to do this, because you're like a brother to me and I've tried to stick by you through everything, but here's the way it has to be. If you mosey on up to Austin and everything goes the way it always does with you, and you come back engaged after one romp in the sack, you'll have to find yourself another best man this time."

A cold chill washed over Mark. He'd known Sam all his life, and when he set his jaw like that, he was deadly serious. Apparently he'd had enough. To be honest, Mark couldn't blame him.

"I ran into Deborah at the grocery store last night," Sam said casually. "You know, it's a wonder she didn't sue you for breach of promise."

"You're right. She had grounds." He glanced nervously at Sam. "Is she still upset?" He was hoping that six months had soothed her feelings.

"I would say she's still upset. She asked if you'd contracted any deadly diseases yet. I think she's sticking pins in a voodoo doll or something."

"So she's not over it."

"Doesn't look like it." Sam signaled to the waitress and glanced at Mark. "Want another beer?"

"I think I'm gonna need one if we're discussing Deb." He waited until Sam had put in their order for two more long-necks. "So what else did she say about me?"

"Oh, the usual. That you're a pimple on the backside of humanity, a virus on the Internet of life. That kind of thing. From the look in her eyes, she was thinking even worse insults than that, but I think she held back because she knows I'm your best friend and we were in a public place."

"I really was hoping she'd be over it by now." He was a rat, no doubt about it. Whenever he thought of how he'd left her high and dry, he used similar expressions to describe himself.

"Well, she's not over it, but she's trying to be. In fact, she's linked up with your four other victims."

"I wish you wouldn't use that word."

"I didn't. She did. She said they've formed a support group. Either they'll help each other to heal or they'll figure out a really hideous form of revenge, whichever comes first."

Mark gazed at Sam uneasily. "A support group? You mean with meetings and everything?"

"Why not? There's five of them, so that makes a group."

"I don't know what to think about this." Mark grabbed the bottle the waitress had just set in front of him and took a generous swig. "I mean, that's kind of scary, Sam. Five women plotting against me."

"You should be scared. Scared straight. They've even given themselves a name."

Mark gazed across the table at his buddy. "Do I want to know what it is?"

"Probably not. But I'm going to tell you anyway. They call their group DOA."

Mark choked on his beer. *"Dead On Arrival?"* He coughed and sputtered as he tried to assimilate the information. "Good God, Sam, what are they planning?"

"They just have a sick sense of humor. The letters actually stand for Damn O'Grady's Ass."

"Oh." Mark was relieved, but not a lot.

"I wouldn't ignore the implication of those three letters if I were you. I'm sure they didn't choose them at random. I think Deborah mentioned something about having T-shirts printed up." Sam took a long swallow of his beer.

Mark followed suit. This subject was giving him the willies. He'd felt like a heel each time he'd called off an impending wedding, and he'd certainly wanted his prospective brides to seek comfort in whatever way they could. But he'd never imagined that they'd band together against him.

"I don't think you can afford to screw up again, buddy," Sam said. "It wouldn't be good for your health."

"Well, I'm not going to screw up. Your idea about using *Texas Men* to find a woman who's really suited to me, and me to her, was a damned good one. Charlie and I have been writing back and forth for—what, three months now?"

"About that."

Mark patted his shirt pocket. "I know her better than I ever knew any of the others—until it was too late, that is. I know she's a morning person like me, but she needs her coffee. She's not anal but she likes to keep her place picked up. She loved *Survivor*, hated *Big Brother*. Even her job is perfect for me—an outdoor adventure guide."

"That is one of her good points, I agree. I've said that from the beginning. You kept dating these financial types you met at the office."

"Right. I wasn't working a big enough area. The magazine changed that, and now I have Charlie, who's the exact right mix, sensible on the outside, but black lace and naughty thoughts underneath."

"Hold it. How do you know about the black lace and naughty thoughts?"

Mark had a feeling he'd just revealed too much. In the past few weeks, the correspondence had heated up considerably. "Just a guess. Come to think of it, I probably read too much into her comments."

"Like hell. Come on, Mark. What did she say?"

Time to backpedal, and fast. "Not much, really. I think she's shy, actually. Probably would be slow to warm up." He didn't think that for a minute. From the tone of her most recent letters, she had an instant on switch. He could hardly wait to trip it.

"Uh-huh." Sam's expression was grim. "I get the picture. No wonder you're so ready to meet her. Mr. Happy wants to meet her, too. That's your other problem. You're a washout at celibacy."

He was, but he didn't want to admit that he'd been dreaming about making love to Charlie McPherson for weeks. That would only confirm Sam's opinion that he couldn't go to Austin alone. "This isn't only about sex. We like the same things. Not a single one of my fiancées wanted to go camping with me. Charlie would love to go camping." And he could hardly wait to get her alone in a cozy tent.

"What's this about camping? I thought you were going to ask her to dinner first."

"Well, dinner, or...I don't know. Camping would be nice."

"It would be a disaster! I know you, and you would not stay in your own little pup tent. No. Camping is out. O-U-T, out." Sam took a quick drink of his beer and glared at him.

Mark shrugged. "It was just an idea."

"A bad idea. Some guys can handle getting physical early in the relationship without losing their perspective on the situation. Take me, for instance. I've *never* proposed to a woman after making love to her the first time. With you, it's like an orgasm kills off half your brain cells. One night of nooky and you're headed for the altar. It's the damnedest thing I've ever seen."

"I admit I've made that mistake a few times."

"No kidding."

Mark sighed. "I've always moved too quick on this proposing business. I can see that now."

"Good. Glad to hear it. Then you'll let me go with you to Austin and make sure you don't screw this one up."

The very thought of dragging Sam along made Mark cringe. "Now, Sam, how's that gonna look? No telling what she'll think if I have to bring my best friend along when I go to meet her for the first time. She'll think I don't trust my own judgment, or I'm lacking in confidence. It's the wrong way to start out."

Sam shrugged. "Then do it your way. I'm sure Jack will agree to be your best man. Maybe I'll tell him to bite the bullet and buy a tux. I'd be money ahead if I'd done that instead of renting one each time. And he can forget about writing a wedding toast. Talk about a waste. On the other hand, he should remember to bring a big box of tissues to the ceremony. No, make that two big boxes. One wasn't enough for this last disaster, by the time I'd passed them out to Deborah, her four bridesmaids, her mother, her—"

"Okay, okay! So you're going with me to Austin." But how he'd manage to make a good impression on Charlie under such circumstances was beyond him. It would be a damned awkward visit.

Perhaps he could come up with a good cover story...

Sam smiled. "That's more like it. You know, I could go for a hamburger. Want a hamburger?"

"Sure, why not?"

"I'll go find our waitress."

"Okay." While he was gone Mark started brainstorming. He'd pulled a few excellent stunts in his college days. Like the time he and Sam had both wanted to date the same girl their senior year. Mark had gone in drag to the cafeteria and confided in this girl that Mark O'Grady had spent two years in China learning lovemaking secrets from the geishas. Sam never had a chance after that.

Hey, wait a minute. What if Sam needed a blind date when he went down to Austin? What if he was afraid to ask anybody out, because...because the woman he'd been dating had turned out to be a man. Perfect. So then Mark could ask Charlie to come up with a date for Sam, to get him back on track. While Sam was kept busy with her, Mark could get busy with Charlie. Brilliant.

Sam returned and slid into the booth. "I'm glad you came to your senses about taking me along to Austin."

Mark smiled, feeling much better about the situation now. "I can't have a wedding without you being my best man." That was certainly true. If Sam wasn't standing up at the altar with him, it wouldn't seem like he was really getting married. Of course, he never really *had* gotten married. But this time would be different. He could feel it.

"You sure look perky all of a sudden," Sam said.

"Why wouldn't I? I'm going to meet the woman of my dreams."

Gazing at him over the top of his beer bottle, Sam cleared his throat. "Mark, old buddy, one of your more endearing traits is your eternal optimism. But I want you to entertain the possibility that Charlie is not the one."

"But she is."

"I hope so, but the truth is we might have to put another ad in *Texas Men* and troll for more prospects. Because I'm not—I repeat, *not*—going through this again until I'm convinced that you won't back out at the last minute."

"I'm telling you, I won't back out. Charlie's the real deal."

"That remains to be seen. Go ahead and set up the

weekend, but remember that there will be no getting horizontal with your darling Charlie if I have anything to say about it. You need to get to know her really well before that happens.''

''But I do know her!''

''Only what she tells you in the letters, pal.'' Sam sipped his beer. ''Only what she tells you in the letters.''

2

A WEEK LATER, Charlie tried not to hyperventilate as she stood in front of the three-way mirror in Ashley's shop. The plunging neckline of the red dress nearly reached her belly button. If she had the nerve to buy this dress, it would go perfectly with some red high-heeled sandals she'd seen in a store window down the street.

She'd never owned anything like this dress in her life, but it fit the image she was trying to project for Saturday night's date with Mark. The longer she wore the dress, the more she believed in her seductive powers.

"Way too daring," Ashley said.

"No, I think this might be the one." Charlie turned this way and that to see if she looked sufficiently sexy. "But I wish it had a slit up the side."

"It used to." Ashley pulled a blue dress off the rack. "When I saw you eyeing that one the other day, I stitched it up. There's such a thing as over-exposed. Even so, that dress is cut way lower than I thought. Try this one instead." She held out the blue dress.

Charlie glanced at it. "Nope. It has sleeves."

"Try it." Ashley shoved the dress closer. "It matches your eyes."

"Who cares? All my life I've been wearing blue because it matches my eyes. And you know what that dress is? *Boring.* I will never get Mark to drool if I wear that. I'll look like Alice in Wonderland. I might as well tie a blue bow in my hair."

"You wear that red number and he'll drool, all right. I'm worried about what will happen after the drooling part."

Charlie turned to face her sister. "Okay, let's get to the bottom of this. Why are you so paranoid about the possibility that Mark and I will have sex on the first date?"

Ashley avoided her gaze and hung the blue dress on the circular rack. "Because I'm your older sister, and older sisters are supposed to keep their little sisters away from the Big Bad Wolf. At least on the first date."

"That's weak and you know it. What's the deal here?"

Ashley rummaged through the rack some more, but finally she turned, her cheeks rosy. "Remember Jason Danville?"

Charlie searched her memory. "Was he the guy who drove the Jaguar?"

Ashley nodded. "When he asked me out, I was the envy of every girl in my sorority. He was older, sophisticated, rich."

"And you went to bed with him on the first date," Charlie guessed.

"On the first and only date." She sighed. "It was so humiliating that I never told anybody. Of course *he* probably told the world. It was so classic. We drank martinis and he convinced me that I was the girl he'd been waiting for all his life. Of course afterward he laughed and called me naive for believing that old line."

"Oh, Ashley." Charlie walked over and gave her sister a hug. "But Mark's not like that," she said. "He would never—"

"Maybe not." Ashley held her by the shoulders. "But don't forget I was there when Kevin Jasper turned you down for the Sadie Hawkins dance back in high school. The way you talk about Mark reminds me of the way you used to talk about Kevin. Come to think of it, you haven't been this excited about a guy since Kevin."

Charlie had to admit that was true. Maybe she hadn't liked being treated like a buddy by the men she'd gone out with, but she hadn't cared enough to try and change the dynamics, either.

"I know you, Charlie," Ashley said. "When your dreams are smashed, you don't recover so well. If Mark turned out to be a rat like Jason, I'd never forgive myself if I let you get hurt."

Charlie appreciated her sister's concern, but she knew it wasn't needed in this instance. Mark wasn't going to hurt her. Still, she wasn't above using an opening when it presented itself. "Okay, then like I asked you before, come with me Saturday night. You'll be able to make a judgment about Mark, help protect me and meet a new guy, all at the same time."

Ashley smiled. "You can stop pushing for the double date. You don't need protection if you drive yourself to the restaurant and drive yourself home, like we talked about, and don't take any side trips in between."

"Maybe he'll slip something in my drink."

"You don't believe that any more than I do. He's a stockbroker at the firm he claimed to be associated with—his letters of reference checked out. He won't do anything weird. But that red dress sends a definite signal, and we don't really know what this guy's agenda is. This three months of letter writing could be a technique to get you in bed."

If Ashley wanted to believe that, Charlie didn't care. It suited her purposes. "And you can keep me from getting carried away by the moment."

Ashley groaned. "Come on, Charlie. Wear a different dress and we don't have to worry. Sure, I feel sorry for this Sam person, but I don't think it's my job to toddle along on your date with you and try to rehabilitate Mark's friend."

"But, Ashley, can you imagine how traumatized he must be? Here he thought he was going out with a perfectly nice woman, and she turned out to be a man."

"I grant you that it might be difficult getting back into dating after something like that, but I—"

"And he didn't discover it until he started making love to her—I mean, *him*," Charlie said. "What a shock! And now the poor guy won't so much as go to dinner with a woman, let alone get sexually involved with someone. Doesn't that pull at your heartstrings?"

Ashley turned back to the rack and began sorting through it. "Well, sure. But he probably needs counseling, not a date with me."

"Mark said he won't go to counseling, but he said if I could just find Sam a nice girl so that we could have a double date, then maybe he will start to trust again. You're the perfect person to go with us Saturday night. Sherry and Dawn are both involved with someone, and I think Ellie's too aggressive for something this delicate. Besides, I want you to go. I'd like you to meet Mark."

"And I will." Ashley paused to look at a black dress, then rejected it and kept scooting dresses around the circular chrome bar. "But this double-date thing seems so contrived."

"Maybe, but Mark says it's the only thing he can figure out. I think it's sweet that he cares so much for his friend, don't you?"

"I suppose. Here, how about this one?" She took a white dress off the rack and held it up.

"*White?* You want him to think I'm virginal?"

"White can be very effective on blondes. I wish I could wear it."

Charlie rolled her eyes. "I don't even want to hear about it, Miss Everybody-Thinks-I'm-a-Model. Every single outfit in this store looks good on you. So white isn't your best color. Big deal. You'd still look glamorous, even in unflattering white. As for me, this red dress is the first thing I've ever tried on that didn't make me look cute. I'm tired of guys wanting to pat me on the head."

"So you're an ingenue type. There's nothing wrong with that."

"But I want them to pat me somewhere else for a change!"

"You can think about that on your second date." Ashley returned the white dress to the rack and found a pink one. "In the meantime, this will—"

"Ick! *Pink.* Barf-o-rama. Pink is exactly what I'm trying to get away from. Just once in my life, I want to knock a guy for a loop the first time he sees me. I don't want him to think, *Hey, I'll bet she plays a good game of tennis.* I want him to go, *Hey, I want a little one-on-one with that hot babe.*"

Ashley folded the pink dress over her arm and gazed at Charlie. "Then that's the dress."

"I thought so."

"But as your big sister, I can't in good conscience let you go to a restaurant alone to meet some guy you've only written letters to. If something awful happened I'd feel responsible because I was the one who dolled you up like that."

"So you'll go along and be Sam's date?"

"I will, but I'm only going to keep an eye on you in that dress. If my being there tricks Sam into finally having a 'date,' then I suppose I can live with that. Just so you and Mark don't expect this foursome to be a regular thing."

"Oh, Ashley, you're terrific! I knew I could count on you." Charlie threw both arms around her sister in an enthusiastic hug.

"I'm a sucker, that's what." Ashley's resigned expression changed to a frown as she stepped back and looked at Charlie. "Rule Number One. No hugging in that dress."

"Why not?"

"Take a look."

Charlie glanced down, and sure enough, one of her breasts had nearly sprung free of the plunging neckline. She grinned as she glanced at Ashley. "This is *such* a sexy dress."

Ashley gave her a stern look. "See that you keep it on."

AS MARK HANDED HIS CAR KEYS to the valet at the restaurant Saturday night, he was still trying to figure out how to tell Sam that Charlie's sister, Ashley, would be coming as Sam's date. He didn't think it was necessary to go into the transvestite story he'd cooked up, first of all because Sam might fail to see the humor in it, and secondly because he couldn't imagine either Charlie or Ashley would bring up the subject. They'd just be extra nice to Sam, which wouldn't hurt a thing.

He didn't like telling untrue stories about Sam, but this meeting with Charlie was so important. If she started thinking he needed a handler to keep him on a tight leash, as if he were some sort of lust-crazed maniac, that could give a bad impression. Likewise, he'd need to think of something to tell Sam that would explain why Charlie's sister was coming to dinner with them.

They'd left Houston in plenty of time to check into a hotel not far from the restaurant and then made it to the restaurant several minutes early. He'd clue Sam in before the women showed up. He just needed to figure out what to say. A beer would help both of them, but that wouldn't look so good, to be starting on the drinks before the women even arrived.

"Seems like a nice place," Sam commented as they walked toward a carpeted entryway covered with a green canopy. Flowers spilled out of stone planters and classical-looking nude statues stood sentry on either side of the glass doors. "But trust you to find the restaurant with naked women standing outside it."

"I had no idea," Mark said.

"Right."

"No, really. I got a recommendation from somebody at work." Mark thanked the doorman as they walked into the restaurant.

"In any case, Italian's usually a safe choice for a first date," Sam said. "Most people can find something to eat, even if they're picky."

"Charlie's not picky," Mark headed for the tuxedo-clad maître d'. "But I wanted something romantic. They're supposed to have a couple of strolling violinists and a flower girl who hands out long-stemmed roses to the women."

"That's a nice touch." Sam brushed a piece of lint from the lapel of his sport coat. "But I should warn you that just because a woman says she's not picky doesn't mean she's not. I've heard that line a million times, and then you take them out for sushi and they refuse to eat it."

"Well, when Charlie says she's not picky, I believe her." Mark glanced through the arched doorway into the dining room and was satisfied with what he saw. High, narrow windows looked out on a garden setting with twinkling white lights strung on the greenery. Inside, candles flickered on linen-draped tables and the chairs were upholstered in a soft green material that looked like velvet.

"And you told her I was coming, right?" Sam asked.

"Sure did." Mark listened for the violinists and, sure enough, he could hear them, but they were very soft. Good. Soft was better.

"Did you tell her why I was coming?"

Mark paused just short of the maître d's station. Time for his fast shuffle routine. "What do you mean?"

"I'm assuming that in all this letter writing you two have been doing, that you've mentioned your little problem with the five previous engagements."

"We haven't gotten into that, specifically, but—"

"You haven't?" Sam's jaw dropped. "Why wouldn't you? Any woman who gets involved with you should know about that small matter, don't you think?"

Mark glanced around nervously. "Keep your voice down, okay? Let's just get seated, and then we'll talk about it."

"Oh, we'll talk about it, all right. I have plenty to say on the subject."

Moments later they were ushered to a table for four in a secluded corner of the room.

Mark chose a chair facing the doorway so he'd know the minute Charlie arrived. "I think you should sit across from me."

"I don't. I think I should sit next to you so I can give you a swift kick under the table whenever necessary." He started to take the chair on Mark's right.

Mark grabbed his arm. "No, you need to sit across from me. Charlie's bringing her sister."

Sam looked at him in astonishment. "She's doing *what?*"

"Bringing her sister. The poor woman. She has this terrible problem. Whenever she's attracted to a guy, she breaks out in a rash. But she seems to be getting better, and Charlie thought it was time to test her recovery. She thought it would be better if Ashley, that's her name, started with a blind date."

Sam's jaw tensed, but he moved to the seat opposite Mark. "I'm not here to be Charlie's sister's blind date."

"I realize that, but when Charlie heard you were coming, she naturally thought about Ashley and her problem."

Sam pulled his chair in and leaned his elbows on the table. "Okay, let's get back to the original question. If Charlie doesn't know I'm here to ride herd on you, why does she think I'm coming?"

Mark shrugged. "As a friend, to meet the woman I've been raving about."

"Hmm." Sam smoothed his mustache. He didn't look particularly convinced. "There's something fishy about all of this, O'Grady. And you can be sure I'll find out what it is eventually."

Mark knew he wouldn't be able to fool Sam for long,

but he only needed to have his cooperation for the next few hours. "All right, maybe I thought it would be kind of cool if you and Charlie's sister hit it off. One big happy family, right?"

Sam continued to look skeptical. "But according to you, if Ashley and I hit it off, then she'll break out in a rash."

"Maybe not. Maybe the hypnosis sessions are working. But don't bring up the subject, okay? She's very sensitive about it."

"Hmm," Sam said again, his gaze speculative.

"What?"

"I'm thinking about some of the stunts you pulled in college. This dinner setup has the same feel to it. And I—" He paused as a waiter arrived to fill their water goblets. "And I still want to know why you haven't told Charlie about all your prior engagements," he said after the waiter left.

"I'll tell her. I promise I'll tell her soon." Mark kept glancing toward the door. Charlie had mentioned she'd be wearing red, and that the dress was cut low in the front, just for him. He loved knowing that. "I wanted to get this first meeting out of the way, so that she'd understand how sincere I am. If she found out about my five engagements before meeting me, it might color everything."

"It damn well should color everything. Then she'd know to take things slow and not go jumping into bed with you. You can't handle it."

"But, Sam, we've been taking it slow. We've been writing letters for three months. That's why this was such a great idea, the magazine thing and then the long correspondence. Now we know each other well enough to take our relationship to the next level."

Sam scowled across the table at him. "You're not changing levels on my watch. This will be a zipless weekend, buddy."

Mark sighed.

"It's for your own good. And hers."

"You're right. I know you're right." No matter how confident he felt this time, his record in such matters was lousy. And he didn't want to hurt Charlie. She already meant so much to him. Of course, if she meant so much to him, then there was no way he'd hurt her, because he'd go through with the ceremony.

"Come on, pal. What's one night compared to a whole lifetime?"

"Good point. Okay, I will not make love to Charlie this weekend. Maybe just a kiss or two. That wouldn't cause a problem. Just –" His breath caught. *There she was.* Oh, damn, she was gorgeous. And so hot. The red dress hugged her curves and swooped down in front to show off the sweetest cleavage he'd ever been privileged to ogle. Damn. He couldn't imagine how he'd keep his hands to himself, his zipper zipped. But he had to. He would. He *would*.

Their waiter was ready to escort her and a stunning brunette to the table, but Charlie spoke to him and the waiter paused.

Smart girl, Mark thought. She wanted to check out her date before the maître d' brought her over. If Mark turned out to be the Hunchback of Notre Dame or The Wolfman, then she could still leave. His Charlie was no dummy.

He stood and started toward her.

She scanned the room and when her gaze settled on him, her smile nearly caused his heart to stop beating. Adrenaline made him shaky as he approached. Seeing her picture hadn't prepared him for her megawatt smile or eyes that sparkled like the waters of the Gulf on a sunny day.

He glanced quickly at the waiter. "I'll escort them over," he said.

"As you wish, sir." The waiter nodded and walked away.

Mark's gaze settled on Charlie again and he couldn't stop grinning. Even her ears were sexy. Before Charlie, he hadn't been a fan of short hair, but with ears that cute, he could see the advantage. He wanted to nibble each diamond-studded lobe while he whispered sweet nothings to his Charlie.

"Hello, Mark." Her voice trembled just enough to tell him how excited she was.

"Hello, Charlie." He wasn't sure what to do next. He wanted to bury his fingers in her blond, wavy hair, tilt her head back and kiss that plump mouth covered in tomato-red lipstick to match her dress. But that probably wasn't a good idea right here in the middle of the restaurant. Besides, if a kiss or two was all he was allowed tonight, he needed to pace himself. "You're...beautiful," he said. "So beautiful."

"Thank you." Her cheeks grew pink. "You're quite the treat, yourself." Then she extended her hand. "Nice to meet you at last, Mark."

He took her warm, soft hand in both of his and held it as if he'd never let go. She was unbelievable. And that dress... His mouth grew moist and his groin tightened. "I'm sorry we waited three months," he said.

"We were trying to be sensible, I guess."

"That was stupid."

"Maybe." She gazed into his eyes for a moment longer before slowly easing her hand from his and shifting her attention to the brunette standing next to her. "Mark, I'd like you to meet my sister, Ashley McPherson."

He'd been so absorbed in Charlie that he'd practically forgotten about Ashley. Now that he took a good look at Charlie's sister, he wanted to laugh with pleasure. Sam was going to thank him for this day.

Ashley was tall, at least five-eight, but Sam was six-two, so no problem there. Her hair reminded him of a Cherry Coke—rich brown with red highlights—and she had green eyes. Green eyes were a particular weakness of Sam's. He wasn't averse to a dynamite figure, either. Yep, he would bless the day his good buddy Mark had set him up with Charlie's sister.

Well, he might not be thrilled about the stories Mark had concocted. But once he realized how necessary it had been in order to start Mark off on the right foot with Charlie, then old Sam would come around.

Ashley held out her hand. "Glad to meet you, Mark."

Mark shook her hand enthusiastically. "Ashley, it means so much to me that you agreed to come tonight. And I'm sure it will mean the world to Sam, too. Let's head over to the table and I'll introduce you."

"All right, but first I want to set my ground rules. I'm doing this as a special favor to Charlie, but please don't expect that we'll become a regular foursome."

"Absolutely. I completely understand." He gestured toward the table in the corner. "We're right over here."

As the women threaded their way through the tables with Mark following behind, Sam rose from his chair. Mark wondered if Ashley might be rethinking her comment about ending the foursome tonight. Sam usually attracted women like a magnet.

Of course Ashley also thought Sam had a serious

phobia about women who turned out to be men, but that would be cleared up before too long. The more Mark thought about the idea of Sam and Ashley getting together, the more he liked it. He and Sam were like brothers, so how perfect if they ended up with sisters.

They reached the table, and Mark cleared his throat. "Sam Cavanaugh, I'd like you to meet Charlie and Ashley McPherson. Ladies, this is my best man—uh, I mean my best friend, Sam."

Sam shook hands with Charlie first. "It's a pleasure, Charlie." Then his gaze flicked over her shoulder to lock with Mark's. The message was clear. *Danger. Don't touch.*

Mark gave his buddy a short nod of understanding, which doubled as a pledge to be careful. Charlie's perfume, something spicy and exotic, wafted up to him. Oh, God, it was as if she'd set out to sabotage all his good intentions. Well, he'd have to be strong.

Then Sam shook hands with Ashley. This time he didn't bother to glance at Mark. Nope. All his concentration was fixed on the lovely Ashley in her elegant little black dress. "It's good to meet you," he said.

Mark recognized that tone of voice. Sam never used it unless he was interested in a woman. Hot damn. This was going great. Sam would become mesmerized by Ashley, which would leave Mark free to...well, to do *something* special with Charlie. Not go to bed with her, of course. He cherished her too much to risk jeopardizing their future. But he would love to kiss her...a lot.

"Shall we sit down?" Ashley asked.

Mark snapped to attention. He'd been so busy dreaming and scheming that he'd left them all standing there by the table. His only consolation was that Sam must have been a little dazed by his first glimpse of

Ashley, too, since he hadn't started pulling out chairs for the women, either.

"Yes," Mark said. "By all means." He hurried around to a chair and pulled it away from the table. "Charlie?"

"Thank you." She gave him another one of those dynamite smiles as she walked toward the chair. First she hooked the little red purse she was carrying over the chair by its long rhinestone-studded strap. Then she did that thing that always got Mark hot when he watched women seat themselves. She smoothed the skirt of her dress down over her bottom before she sat down, so she wouldn't wrinkle the material.

Mark loved it when women did that. And to watch Charlie slide both hands over that shiny red material was almost more than he could stand. After her wonderful behind was tucked in securely against the velvet seat, he gripped the back of her chair and scooted her in. That's when he chanced to look down over her shoulder. Oh, Lord. The neckline of her dress was like a curtain drawn back just enough to tease him with the possibilities lurking behind it.

Her breasts, rounded and perky, nestled just barely inside the sweep of red material. He could almost visualize how they'd look, but not quite. Very little material barred him from the view he was after, though. A man wouldn't have to work very hard to coax those treasures out of hiding.

But he'd vowed to limit himself to a couple of kisses. Still, he hadn't decided exactly where those kisses might be placed.... No. He couldn't chance kissing her anywhere but on the mouth. And he'd have to make sure his hands didn't wander, either, no matter how tempting the neckline of that dress was. And it was certainly very tempting....

"Mark?" Sam asked. "Will you be joining us this evening?"

3

ALL HER ADULT LIFE Charlie had dreamed of having a man transfixed by the sight of her cleavage. Yet until tonight, she hadn't had the nerve to dress to attract that kind of attention.

She hadn't even had the nerve to ask a guy to take her to fancy restaurants where plunging necklines would be appropriate. She'd been afraid they'd laugh. Her reputation as a tomboy had preceded her, partly because she met men on the hiking trail, for the most part. Because she was so obviously in her element there, they'd all assumed she preferred pizza parlors to five-star dining.

In general, she did, but she'd always longed for this—to appear in the doorway of an elegant room, to make heads turn as she walked to her table, and to be helped into her place by a fabulous-looking man who couldn't stop looking at her.

Ashley had been very perceptive to bring up Kevin Jasper. Kevin had chosen to go to that dance with someone more glamorous than Charlie, and from that moment on she'd decided her fate was cast. She wasn't the type of girl who could compete in a sophisticated arena.

Yet this time, she'd worked up the courage to try. Because she'd been able to control Mark's perception of her through the letters, she'd been able to indulge her secret longing to become a man's sexual fantasy.

And she'd been able to stage his first impression of her. Instead of meeting him in khaki shorts, T-shirt, hiking boots and backpack, with sweat beading her forehead and no makeup, she could show him this other side of her personality, one that no one understood.

She'd bet her comments about romantic candlelight dinners had prompted him to choose this restaurant. Everything about it thrilled her, from the soft lighting to the strolling violinists. Mark didn't seem to be paying much attention to the restaurant, though. She'd never made a man forget his surroundings before.

And what a man. His shoulders were broader, his rich brown hair thicker and his smile more devastating than she'd ever imagined by looking at his picture. She could write an entire essay on the cute dimple that appeared whenever he smiled, and the way his eyes crinkled at the corners.

And what fascinating eyes. That deep brown turned her knees to jelly, and when she caught the gleam of appreciation and knew it was all for her, she was ready to drag Mark off to the nearest secluded spot and get it on. The dress made her feel almost daring enough to do it, too.

From his reaction to her, he felt the same. His face was even a little red with embarrassment as he took his seat at the table, because he'd been caught ogling.

She flashed him a smile to let him know he hadn't offended her in the least with his preoccupation with her breasts. The attention was new and exciting to her. He could be preoccupied with any part of her he wanted, for as long as he liked.

He grinned back and nudged her knee gently under the table.

She nudged back. Wow, this was cool, playing a little

footsie under the table. No guy had ever been moved to play footsie with her. Touch football, but never footsie. And every time he looked at her, she could tell he was thinking the same thing she was—that they needed to ditch their chaperones and get naked.

She'd achieved her goal. He was definitely, positively drooling. At last she had a man buggy-eyed over her, and it felt great. She was enjoying every second of this triumph.

Ashley, on the other hand, apparently wasn't so enthusiastic about it. Charlie could tell that immediately from the worried sound of her voice.

"Charlie, I seem to have something in my eye," she said. "If you two will excuse us for a minute, I'd like Charlie to come with me to the ladies' room and see if she can find anything."

"Of course." Mark leaped to his feet and grasped Charlie's chair once again.

"No problem." Sam followed suit and helped Ashley out of her chair.

Charlie figured Mark would be more careful not to stare at her chest this time, but at least she could use the opportunity to slide out of her chair in such a way that she brushed up against him. "Thank you," she murmured, turning to give him a subtle wink. "We'll be right back."

"Hope so." He gazed at her with pure relish.

She unhooked her purse from the back of the chair and positioned it over her bare shoulder before following Ashley toward the ladies' room. She had no doubt that Mark would watch her leave. That was a new and exhilarating feeling, too. She believed he had lust in his heart. Mission accomplished.

What a beautiful evening, she thought as she followed Ashley toward the tasteful sign marking the ladies' room. Even the bathroom was gorgeous. The door opened onto a sitting room, and the bathroom lay beyond that. A mural of the Italian countryside ran along the walls, and two green velvet love seats were grouped beneath the mural.

Ashley didn't seem inclined to sit on either one. The minute they were inside the door, she turned to Charlie. "You are scaring me to death!"

"Don't be scared. I'm a big girl."

"That's what I'm afraid of." Ashley reached over and tried to pull the neckline of Charlie's dress together more. "I should never have agreed to let you wear this dress."

"Ashley, if you hadn't been willing to sell me this dress, I would have gone to another dress shop and bought the closest thing to it. I wanted to knock his socks off, and by God, I'm doing it."

"I'm afraid more than his socks are due to come off if you parade around much longer in that dress." She snapped open her small evening purse and began to rummage through it. "I wonder if I brought any safety pins. Maybe we could—"

"I'm not going back out there with my dress pinned together, if that's what you're planning. Please relax. Mark is not like that Jason guy who was so cruel to you. He's the sort of person who cares about people. He cares about Sam, for instance."

Ashley stopped rummaging through her purse looking for safety pins. "Did you hear how he introduced Sam, by the way? At first he called him his best *man*. Then he corrected himself and said he was his best *friend*. What's up with that?"

Charlie smiled. "I'd say he's a guy with marriage on his mind, that's what I'd say. That can't be bad, can it?"

Ashley seemed to be turning that over in her mind. "I guess not." She gazed at Charlie. "I would love it if he turned out to be the guy for you. I really would. But I still don't like the idea of you two rushing into a physical relationship."

"That's not very likely, is it, with our two chaperones in attendance?"

"Good point. Now that you mention that, I'm glad Sam and I are here."

Charlie had been mesmerized by Mark, but she hadn't been totally oblivious to the instant attraction between her sister and Sam. Still she wanted to play it close to the vest. "What do you think of Sam, by the way?"

"Well, he's very good-looking, if that's what you mean. But I can tell he's nervous in this situation."

"I'm not surprised. He doesn't know whether you used to be my brother Adam who turned into my sister Ashley. But eventually he'll probably relax."

"Doesn't really matter." Ashley glanced in an oval mirror hanging over an antique cherry vanity and fluffed her hair. "I doubt I'll see him again."

"Really? Why not?"

"He's got this whole psychological hang-up going on." Ashley pursed her lips, then opened her purse again and took out a tube of lipstick. "I'm really not interested in dealing with that."

Charlie couldn't resist. "Then why are you bothering to redo your lipstick?"

Ashley finished gliding the mocha lipstick over her mouth and twisted it back into its tube. "Habit," she said, dropping the tube back into her purse.

"If you say so."

"And even if I did find him attractive, I wouldn't get so involved that I'd forget why I'm here." Ashley fixed Charlie with a determined gaze. "Now promise me that you won't let that man get you alone tonight. I've been watching him, and his tongue is dragging on the floor. If you give him an opening, he's going to take it."

Charlie thought that sounded pretty darned thrilling.

"It's that gleam in your eye that has me so worried!" Ashley said. "Now please tell me you'll exercise some caution."

"Okay, I'll exercise some caution." She wondered if the condoms in her purse counted. "But you're the one who mentioned his slip of the tongue. If you ask me, Mark and I are practically engaged."

"Oh, then I guess that was a big diamond ring I saw in his pocket."

Charlie laughed. "Ashley, you don't know how long I've waited to get this reaction from a man. No man has ever had an erection just looking at me fully dressed, unless you count Donny Smoggles back in tenth grade, which I don't, considering every girl in school made Donny's little circus tent go up."

Ashley's stern expression dissolved into laughter. "I do remember Donny."

"Is it so wrong to want to make a man totally lose his mind?" She sent her sister a pleading glance.

Ashley studied her for a long moment. "No, I guess not." She sighed. "It's not his mind that concerns me."

"I know," Charlie said with a grin.

"And besides the obvious, I don't want him to break your heart, either."

"He won't. I know he won't."

"I hope you're right. Here. Let me adjust that neckline again."

ONCE THE WOMEN were out of earshot, Sam leaned
across the table. "It's a damned good thing I came
along, buddy boy, or you would be toast. Now, here's
the plan. Under no circumstances are you to continue
looking at her cleavage. Otherwise you are so dead."

Mark laughed in disbelief. "Not look? Are you in-
sane? Why not tell me to do a few gymnastics while
hanging from the chandelier? That would be a hell of a
lot easier."

Sam blew out a breath and leaned back in his chair. "I
get your point, but we've got to neutralize the effect of
that dress."

"Unless you plan to make her wear your sport coat
and put it on backward, I don't know how you're gonna
neutralize anything. I think we'll just have to live with
the situation." Mark wasn't particularly upset with that
prospect. He thought it would be a crime to cover Charlie, sort of like throwing a blanket over one of those
nude statues outside the door.

"Man, I never expected an outdoor adventure guide
to show up in an outfit like that."

Mark decided not to tell Sam that he'd known about
the dress all along. He also knew the color of her panties. Charlie's last letter to him had been filled with spicy
little details like that. They'd been taunting each other
with increasingly erotic messages. No, he'd better not
tell Sam about that.

He decided to ease around to a different topic. "Don't
forget that she is an outdoor adventure guide. Don't
forget all the reasons why you advised me to write to
her. She's everything I hoped for, and then some. To

find out how beautiful and sexy she is in person is icing on the cake, because I was already convinced she was perfect for me."

"I do have a good feeling about this one," Sam admitted. "Still, I'd feel a hell of a lot better if you put off the proposal for as long as possible."

The waiter arrived with leather-bound menus, but Mark left his closed. He didn't really care about the food, anyway. "Tell you what. I'll do my best to ignore her cleavage," he said by way of trying to pacify Sam.

"Like you said, easier said than done." Sam opened his menu.

"I'll do my best. So, what did you think of Ashley?"

Immediately Sam glanced up from his perusal of the menu. Then he tried to look casual and nonchalant, the way he always did when he was intensely interested in a woman. "She's okay." He looked down at the menu again.

"Okay? Just okay? I don't think there's a woman you've dated in the past five years that compares to her. And how about those eyes? Are those the greenest eyes you've ever seen, or what?"

Sam shrugged and continued to examine the menu. "I guess. But what difference does it make? She's not breaking out in a rash, so she must not find me attractive."

Mark thought fast. Sam had a very tender ego, and whenever he thought a woman wasn't returning his interest, he bailed. If a woman played hard to get, then Sam didn't pursue her. He hoped Ashley wasn't into those kinds of games. "Um, I think Charlie said the rash appears on her...cheeks," he said.

"There was no rash on her cheeks."

"Her other cheeks."

Sam looked up. "Oh." He gazed at Mark for a couple of seconds. "That's kind of weird, don't you think?"

"Stress affects everybody differently. She might have dragged Charlie into the ladies' room because her rash was starting to bother her."

Sam closed the menu and laid it beside his plate. "No, she dragged Charlie into the ladies' room because you were starting to bother her. She's protective of her little sister, and I don't blame her."

"There, see? That's a point scored by Ashley right off the bat. She's protective of her family members. You're protective of your family members. I remember when that kid tried to beat up your little brother and you got all over—"

"Let's get back to the subject at hand—which is her rash problem. You told me this rash of hers is a social embarrassment. If it only shows up on her backside, I don't understand how that would be an embarrassment, because nobody except her would even know about it."

"Of course it would be a problem." It was a good thing he was used to dealing with Sam's lawyerly logic. "If she's attracted to someone, that means that eventually she'd want to get physical with them, and yet she couldn't allow that to happen, because then the guy would see her rash."

"Oh." Sam frowned. "I still think there's something fishy about all of this. But in some stupid way, it makes sense. I can't imagine any other reason why a woman who looks like Ashley would agree to a blind date. She should have guys coming out of the woodwork."

"Aha! So you do think she's gorgeous."

"From what I can see. Of course I'm picturing this

rash, and that's not exactly a turn-on, if you get my drift."

Mark was working hard not to laugh. He thought this whole thing was hilarious, and he hoped someday Sam would enjoy the joke as much as Mark did right now. "Maybe she's got the rash situation under control," he said. "Maybe she's very attracted to you, and yet she's not breaking out. If that's the case, you would want to continue to help her along with her recovery, wouldn't you?"

Sam rubbed his chin. "You're up to something, O'Grady. I figure it's based on fixing me up with Ashley so you can sneak off with Charlie and do the nasty."

"Not the nasty." Mark held up both hands when Sam lifted his eyebrows as if he didn't believe a word. "Really. I'm not going to do the nasty. But I'd like to kiss her, at least, which could be difficult if you and Ashley are watching us every damned minute. I wouldn't mind having the two of you talk among yourselves sometime during the evening."

"You plan to start making out with Charlie right here at the table?"

"Of course not! I thought later we might go dancing."

"Dancing? With her in that dress? Or sort of in that dress? I don't think so, Mark, old boy. You would—"

"Whoops, here they come. Now if you want to know if Ashley's attracted to you or not, look at her lipstick. If she globbed some more on while she was in the bathroom, then that means she wants you."

"You've said that before when we were out with women, and I think you're making it up. Women put on lipstick for no reason. They put on lipstick to go to the grocery store, for crying out loud. I never understood that."

"Because they might meet a hot prospect at the grocery store, that's why," Mark said. "Lipstick is part of that whole mating thing. Remember, we saw that on the Discovery Channel. Look at the lipstick."

"How do I know if she put it on for me? Maybe she wants the waiter really bad. Or the maître d', although personally I think he's a little old for—"

"Oh, for God's sake, Sam. I swear you'd make a sow's ear out of a silk purse." Then he got out of his chair so he could help his fabulous Lady in Red into her seat. And his vow not to look at her cleavage didn't last even for a second. But he rationalized that she'd worn the dress on purpose to make him notice, so if he didn't, she'd be disappointed.

He didn't want to disappoint this woman. Not ever. And that was why he would be a good boy tonight and just enjoy the view from a distance.

"Did you get whatever it was out of your eye?" Sam asked Ashley, peering intently at her face.

Mark looked, too, and saw the fresh shine of new lipstick. Way to go, Ashley. Then he glanced over at Charlie and was gratified to see that she'd added more of that tomato-red color to her mouth. He'd ten times rather spend the next hour kissing that plump little mouth than eating pasta.

"My eye's fine," Ashley said. "Probably an eyelash or something."

"I can see how that would happen. Your eyelashes are pretty long," Sam said.

Good, Mark thought. Sam liked long eyelashes. Charlie's eyelashes were long, too, and she had mascara on them. Blondes usually used the stuff, he knew, because without mascara their eyelashes didn't stand out so much.

He'd like to see Charlie without her mascara, though. No doubt she'd look perfectly fine. He'd like to see her without her clothes, too. She'd look more than perfectly fine without her clothes.

But he wouldn't be doing that this weekend. No sir. So he'd content himself with simply sitting and watching Charlie. Somehow he managed to order his meal and make a wine decision, but he couldn't remember his choices thirty seconds after he'd made them.

Charlie totally absorbed his attention. He made small talk. So did she. But the conversation was unimportant. All that mattered was being here together, his knee touching hers, his hand resting on the tablecloth where he could accidentally brush her little finger with his.

Now she was picking up her water goblet. Now she was putting it up to those red lips. Now she was taking a sip. Now she was giving him that coy look that made his pulse hammer. He was vaguely aware that Ashley and Sam were talking to each other, but he wasn't aware of anything they said.

Charlie-watching was becoming his favorite activity. The only problem was that the more he watched, the more aroused he became. Well, too bad. Tonight he would be strong. For her sake.

4

CHARLIE BARELY TASTED HER DINNER. Somehow she had to come up with a way to get her sister and Sam out of the picture so she could be alone with Mark. He was everything she'd hoped and she could hardly wait to get her hands on him.

After all the sexy things they'd said to each other in their letters recently, she was ready for more than heated glances and knees touching under the table. The single rose looked lovely resting beside her plate, and the strolling violinists were romantic, but by the end of the meal she needed more than that.

She wanted to be held, to be kissed, to be caressed. In the process, she'd find out what it was like to touch the dimple on Mark's cheek and feel the texture of his hair beneath her fingers. She might even find out what he looked like without his sport coat, without his tie, or even without...everything. Her body throbbed just thinking about that possibility.

But he'd brought Sam along, and that was the fly in the ointment.

She couldn't really blame him. It had been a decent and kind thing to do, and Sam seemed like a terrific guy, but it sure did make for an awkward situation having him and Ashley hanging around. The meal was drawing to a close and she didn't know what to suggest that would allow her an intimate encounter with Mark.

By the time they were standing outside the restaurant waiting for the valet to bring the cars, she still hadn't thought of a good solution for extending the evening. Inviting them all back to her apartment wasn't a very romantic thought, and they were overdressed for the movies.

Dancing would work, but she wasn't up on the dancing scene in Austin, even though she was a decent dancer. Her other dates hadn't thought she'd be into that, so she hadn't spent much time nightclubbing.

She glanced at Mark in silent appeal. The evening couldn't end now. It just couldn't.

He met her gaze and his eyes were filled with the same longing. Then he looked over at Sam. "I hate to call it a night so soon, don't you? Our hotel has a lounge with a live band and a small dance floor, so we could—"

"Great idea," Charlie said. At last a man had pictured her as an inviting dance partner. And she'd get to put her arms around him, at least while the music played. That was a beginning. "Isn't it a great idea, Ashley?"

"No!" said Ashley and Sam together.

Charlie seized the moment. "Then I have the perfect solution. We have two cars here. Mark and I can take one of them and go dancing, and Sam and Ashley can take the other one and do...whatever they want."

"On the other hand, dancing might be a good idea," Ashley said quickly.

"Sure," Sam added. "I could tag along for some dancing for a little while. Then Mark and I should probably turn in. Big day tomorrow."

"On Sunday?" Charlie asked.

"Oh, yeah. We're both behind at work, right, buddy?"

"Uh, right, Sam."

"Right." Sam sent a meaningful glance in Mark's direction. "So you and I can lead and the women can follow us over."

"Oh, for God's sake." Mark faced his friend. "This is getting ridiculous. I don't care how we divvy up the car situation, except that I plan to ride over with Charlie."

Charlie wanted to punch the air in victory.

"We only have a little time together," Mark continued, "and I don't want to waste it going in separate cars."

Sam considered that for a minute. "Okay, Ashley and I will take your Lexus."

"Fine." He started toward Charlie's little red Miata and paused. "How come?"

Ashley gestured to the two cars lined up in front of the restaurant. "Even I know why. Here we have your car, a luxury sedan, a make-out car if I ever saw one, with plush seats in front *and back.* Over here we have Charlie's car, a two-seater sports car. Try to make out in that and you'd need a chiropractor." She glanced at Sam. "Nice to know we're both on the same page."

Sam grinned at her. "Yeah, isn't it?"

"You guys are worse than parents!" Charlie said, hardly able to believe they were having this conversation. "Listen, Ashley, I have to agree with Mark on this one. The heavy-duty chaperone routine is getting ridiculous. Mark and I are adults. We don't have to be protected from each other, right, Mark?"

To her surprise, instead of backing her up, Mark hesitated. Then his face reddened. "Uh—of course not, but I'm sure Sam and Ashley have good intentions."

"I'm sure they do, too. Just misguided."

Sam looked amused. "Well, Ashley, let's take our

misguided intentions and drive to the hotel in Mark's Lexus. You can keep an eye on the rearview mirror." He opened the passenger door for her.

"You're a man after my own heart." She smiled and got into the car.

"Whatever." Charlie threw up her hands and looked at Mark. He was still gorgeous, but she was a little put out with him. He hadn't supported her bid to be alone. "Shall I drive or do you want to?"

"Let him drive," Sam called out before he climbed into the Lexus. "It'll keep his hands busy."

Mark gave her a sheepish grin. "You know, he's probably right. That dress really is tempting."

Charlie thought about that and was somewhat mollified. In a way, she liked knowing that Mark was worried about controlling himself with her, even on the short drive to the hotel. She'd never caused a man to be that wild and crazy. That everyone was so concerned about his ability to restrain himself was a boost to her ego, come to think of it.

She headed for the passenger side of her little Miata. "Okay," she said. "You can drive." When Mark helped her in, she gave his hand a squeeze and gazed up at him. His attention was firmly fastened on her breasts. "Thanks," she murmured.

He glanced at her and swallowed. "You're welcome."

Excitement curled in her tummy. She wanted to kiss him so much she could barely stand it. "We could always ditch our watchdogs."

"I—no, we'd better not. Sam would get worried and call the police. We'll just...go dancing."

She decided to settle for that, but she hoped he meant slow dancing. Very slow.

Mark rounded the car and climbed in, although his knees nearly hit the dashboard of the small car. "Tight fit."

"The seat moves back a little."

"Good." He adjusted the seat, and even so he looked a little cramped in her tiny car.

Personally Charlie liked the close quarters. Mark was within easy reach. She gazed at his profile and could barely believe that he was here. The scent of his aftershave teased her with possibilities.

"I guess you think Sam's concern is a little over the top," he said as he pulled out and followed the Lexus down the road. "But he means well."

Charlie sighed. "So does Ashley. She said writing to each other for three months isn't the same as dating for three months."

"Sam said the same thing."

Wow, this was cozy. Charlie wished the drive would take a while, but she knew they weren't far away from the hotel. "Is there any chance Sam is letting his own little problem get in the way of your dating life?"

"Problem?"

"You know. Maybe he thinks I'll suddenly turn out to be a man, too." She focused on Mark's lips. They were *so* tempting. No doubt he was a good kisser. You could tell those things by the look of a man's mouth.

"Oh, *that* problem. No, I don't think he believes that about you or Ashley. In fact, from the way he's acting with Ashley, I think he's getting over his phobia."

"Good. Then maybe he'll leave us alone." *So I can start kissing you.*

Mark laughed. "Don't count on it. But I can't get too upset with him. He's always been there for me."

"Yeah, exactly." Charlie grinned. "And that's where

he is right now. *There.*" She loved watching Mark's hands on the steering wheel and imagining them elsewhere....

"He doesn't want either of us to get hurt, that's all. And he's invested in making this work out for us. I've been through a few...experiences with women who were all wrong for me. He's the one who first suggested the *Texas Men* thing."

"Is he?" Charlie was feeling more mellow toward Sam already, knowing that. Now if only he'd go away. "Then I'll have to thank him."

"I've thanked him on a regular basis ever since you and I started writing to each other. I really do owe the guy, and it's true that he's worried that I'll move too fast with you. I've sort of promised him that I won't...I mean, that this first night, you and I won't..."

She reached over and slid her hand down his thigh. Her heart hammered as she felt the muscles tighten. "That we won't make love?"

He groaned. "Yep, and I'm in big trouble already. I thought I could manage just a dinner and maybe some dancing, maybe even a nightcap, and then let you go home. But I'm about to combust."

"I'm glad." She squeezed his thigh and took her hand away. "That was my intention."

"Seriously?"

"Seriously." And now was as good a time as any to state her case. She took a deep breath. "You never asked why I wrote to you in the first place—why I decided to answer an ad in *Texas Men.*"

"No, I guess I never did." He glanced at her. "So tell me."

"All my other relationships with men have been so...predictable. We'd meet on the trail or through friends, have a coffee date, have a lunch date, go on a few hikes, maybe, or play tennis once or twice. Then we'd do dinner a few times. Then finally we'd consider the matter of spending the night together. Often by that time I'd be so bored out of my tree I'd say to heck with the whole business."

His voice was husky. "I'm glad to hear it. I'm overjoyed to hear it. I don't like to think of you with anybody else."

"Mark, don't get me wrong. I'm not a virgin."

"That's okay. I just don't want anybody else to count."

She took satisfaction in the tense set of his jaw. He was already getting possessive about her. She liked that. "They don't count. Because there was no real excitement. I thought, by teasing you a bit in the letters, that when we finally met it would be dynamite."

"Well, that sure worked, especially with that dress to cap it off."

"But don't you see?" She had to make him understand. "If we do the dancing thing, and the nightcap thing, and then you go up to your hotel room and I go back to my apartment, it'll be like somebody threw water on the fuse!"

"No, it won't," he said with feeling. "I don't know about your fuse, but mine isn't about to go out. I think my fuse is permanently lit."

"Mark, listen to me. I want wild. I want reckless. I want unrestrained. Just once in my life."

"Couldn't you have all that next weekend? We could go camping, and then—"

She groaned. No way could she be a *femme fatale* when they went camping. "If we wait until next weekend, this will be like my other experiences with men."

"I beg to differ!"

"Well, it would feel like it, anyway. Sensible. Cautious. *Boring*." She slid her hand over his thigh again. "You don't want us to be boring, do you, Mark?"

His breathing rasped in the confines of the small car. "Oh, Lord. Oh, Lord, Lord, Lord."

"Just go with the flow."

"Charlie, it's kind of like a point of honor with me." He sounded desperate. "I've been known to rush into a physical relationship."

"I don't call this rushing, do you?"

"Well, maybe not, but I still think it would be good for me to get through this first date without—"

"Just relax." She stroked his thigh again and knew he was anything but relaxed. "Everything will work out."

"It has to."

"It will." She looked up ahead to where the Lexus was turning in to the entry of the hotel. "Well, here we are. Dancing will be nice."

Mark sounded short of breath. "Dancing will be torture."

She smiled. They were going dancing at a hotel. Hotels had lots of rooms and lots of beds. She had a feeling that she and Mark would get wild and crazy, just the way she'd hoped, before the night was over. He might be gun-shy because he'd made love with other women too quickly and been burned, but he hadn't been writing to other women for three months. He would be fine with her.

The Lexus came to a stop at the hotel entrance where lights from the portico illuminated its shiny black paint job, along with some white smudges on the back window.

"What's that on the back window of your car?" she asked.

Mark coughed. "What do you mean?"

"It looks like white paint, as if something was lettered on it."

"Uh, yeah, some guys painted a message on there, for a joke. They were smashed at the time and got the wrong kind of paint. I haven't been able to clean it all off yet. I need to buy some special solvent."

"The first letter looks like a *J*. What does that stand for?"

"Believe me, you don't want to know."

Charlie tried to think of an obscene word that started with a J. Nothing came to mind. "Oh, well. I'll bet you'll be glad when you finally get it all cleaned off, huh?"

"Yep. I most certainly will."

"So, DID YOU TELL HER YET?" Sam asked as he and Mark stood at the bar waiting for the drinks they'd ordered for the four of them. The women were ensconced at a table near the minuscule dance floor. Both Sam's and Mark's jackets hung on the backs of the two empty chairs and their ties had been stuffed into the pockets in preparation for some serious dancing.

But the band had taken a break the moment they'd arrived, and none of the customers had chosen to dance to the recorded music flowing through the lounge's sound system. Consequently the cocktail waitress was very busy and Mark had suggested getting their own drinks while they waited for the band to come back.

"Well, did you?" Sam prompted.

Mark didn't have to ask what he meant. "I need some peace and quiet alone with her to explain that," he said. "But, for the record, as we drove up she noticed that somebody had painted something on the back window of my car."

"Now, see? That was the perfect time to tell her."

"Oh, yeah, sure. We were about to get out of the car and join you guys. How could I throw something like that at her without having time to explain?"

"I still say it was the perfect opening. You could have signaled to me that you needed time to talk with her. I would have picked up on that."

Mark rubbed the back of his neck. "It's not the kind of thing you can explain in five minutes. Think about it. People don't paint *Just Married* on the back window of your car until right before the wedding. I'd have to start the whole crummy story by giving her the worst scenario first. I want to lead up to the Deborah disaster. And I'd really like Charlie to be totally in love with me before I tell her about Deb. I think she'd take it better."

"I'm not sure I agree with you."

"Look, Sam, I gotta do this part my way. Not making love tonight—I'm willing to go along on that. It won't be easy holding off, but I'm committed to it. As for telling her about those five broken engagements, that's something I have to do in my own time, when I feel it's right."

Sam glanced over at the table and then back at Mark. "Okay. But you'd better keep her out of Houston until you spill the beans. You'd be amazed how word's gotten around."

"Compliments of the DOA Support Group?"

"I'll admit they've been busy."

Mark scowled at him. "Did they buy you a T-shirt?"

"They did, but I told them that out of friendship for you I couldn't wear it." He grinned. "At least not yet. So try and stay on my good side, okay?"

"Hey, I introduced you to Ashley and bought you dinner." Mark paid the bartender before handing Sam one of the beers and Ashley's glass of Chardonnay, each with a cocktail napkin underneath. "Now I'm even buying you this drink. What more do you want from me?"

"A wedding that actually takes place."

"I'm working on that." Mark picked up his own beer and Charlie's glass of Merlot. "How's it going with Ashley?"

"We had sort of a strange conversation on the way over."

Mark held his breath. Now was not the time he wanted his little subterfuge to be revealed. He forced himself to relax. "Really? About what?"

"Transvestites, of all things. She wanted me to know that she doesn't approve of them pretending to be women and trying to pick up straight guys. I told her I wasn't big on that, either, but it was kind of weird that she'd choose that topic."

Mark tried to look casual. "Maybe she read something about it in one of those women's magazines. They're putting all kinds of things in those magazines these days. It's way beyond makeup and clothes."

"Could be. Anyway, she's not fond of lawyers in general, but she seems to be willing to make an exception in my case. I'll bet that's partly because she knows I'm trying to keep you and Charlie from getting horizontal."

Mark panicked. "You didn't tell her why, did you?"

"No. That's your job, not mine."

Mark let out his breath. "So how do you feel about Ashley?"

"I could stand to see her again," Sam said with studied nonchalance.

Mark laughed. "From the master of understatement, I'll take that to mean that you're hooked."

"I have to admit this is turning out better than I expected. But I don't think she's developing a rash. She's not squirming around or anything."

"I'm sure the rash problem is cured, because she does seem to be into you."

"You think so?" Sam looked pleased.

"I think so. Now, come on. The band's ready to play again, and I want to dance with my girl."

As they approached the table, the band launched into a fast number. Mark had been picturing something slow that allowed him to hold Charlie close, so he considered suggesting they sit this one out.

Charlie preempted him by leaving her chair as he deposited their drinks on the table. "Let's dance," she said.

"Sure." He wasn't about to refuse her if that's what she wanted. And maybe some rapid movement would work the tension out of his system.

He hadn't considered Charlie's rapid movement, which only added tension in his system. Her breasts quivered seductively. He was amazed that they stayed tucked inside the dress, but somehow, either by her efforts or the wonders of modern fashion, they did. And then he had to deal with the rhythm of her hips, and the look in her eyes, which had gone all smoky blue and mysterious. She was definitely taunting him.

As she danced, her lips parted and a tiny drop of moisture gathered in the hollow of her throat. He wanted to lick it off. He could almost taste the salt on his tongue. After he'd lapped up that single glistening drop, he'd run his tongue along the swooping neckline of her dress, over the inviting swell of her breast, and then...

"Mark, you're not dancing!" she said with a laugh.

He looked down at his feet, the way he used to when he was thirteen and just learning. And sure enough, his feet had stopped moving. He glanced back up and shrugged. "Batteries must be low." Then he grinned and started dancing again.

This had to be love. It had to be what he'd waited a lifetime to find. He'd never been out on the floor with a woman and totally forgotten to dance. Charlie was powerful medicine, all right.

By concentrating very hard on what he was doing, he managed to keep himself moving for the rest of the number. Between remembering to dance and trying to discipline his thoughts so he wouldn't get an erection, he was a busy man.

Eventually the music stopped, and he led Charlie back to their table in a state of semi-arousal that had threatened to become chronic. Ashley and Sam had also returned from the floor, both of them laughing and breathing hard. Mark hadn't even noticed they were out there, and it wasn't a large area. As he sat down he glanced around and noticed two couples remained standing, waiting for the next number, while another pair had returned to their seats. That dance floor must have been crowded, and he'd felt as if he and Charlie were all alone.

Yep, he had it bad.

Charlie picked up her glass of wine. "Here's to us," she murmured.

He touched his beer mug to her glass. "Here's to the U.S. Mail."

"I'd rather drink a toast to one particular U.S. male."

She eyed him over the rim of her goblet and smiled. "And I'll bet you deliver." Holding his gaze, she sipped the red wine. Then she lowered the glass. A drop of ruby liquid trembled on her lower lip, and she licked it away with a slow swipe of her pink tongue.

Mark's chest grew tight and the erection he'd been trying to control all night threatened to make itself obvious.

"Hey, you guys want some pretzels?" Sam asked, shoving a bowl in Mark's direction.

"No, thanks." Mark realized that his voice sounded like a bullfrog's. He cleared his throat. "Charlie? Want some pretzels?"

The band moved into a slower song.

"I'd rather dance," she said.

"Sure." Anything. Anything she wanted. Well, except making love. But he had a feeling that was the single most important thing she wanted right now.

5

CHARLIE THOUGHT she should be able to work this one out. She'd always been a leader. She'd led whole groups of people through rapids, up steep trails, into dark caves. She should be able to lead one sexually aroused man to bed. But apparently Sam had convinced him it wasn't a good idea.

That in itself was a fascinating concept. From her understanding of men, guys usually encouraged their friends to go for it. She had several male friends who thought of her as a buddy more than a prospective date, and maybe because of that they'd never edited their comments when she was around. From their conversations, she'd gathered that the sooner they could have sex with a woman who turned them on, the better.

She knew she turned Mark on. The trick was to convince him to do something about it. As she moved into the circle of Mark's arms, she hoped a long, slow, exchange of body heat on the dance floor might be all the convincing he would need.

His muffled groan as he pulled her close sounded encouraging.

He smelled so damned good. She breathed in his aftershave and buried her fingertips in his silky hair as she nestled her cheek against his. Her three-inch heels created the perfect alignment for brushing her pelvis across the ridge pushing at the material of his slacks. "This is nice."

"This is hell," he murmured against her ear. "I keep thinking of those black lace panties you told me you'd wear tonight. Did you?"

"Uh-huh."

"Oh, Lord."

"That black lace is quite damp, now," she whispered. "Very damp."

"You're killing me. I hope you know that."

"No, I'm seducing you."

"And you're doing a first-class job." He wrapped both arms around her. "Do you realize I haven't even kissed you yet?"

She leaned back to look into his eyes, and the desire she saw there raised her pulse rate another few notches. "Want to kiss me now?"

"Yes. But I'm afraid I'll lose it if I do."

"Chicken."

His gaze drifted to her mouth. "The thing is, once I start kissing you, I might not stop."

"I'll help you. We'll control it." She ran a fingertip over his lower lip and her breath caught. His mouth reminded her of the full-lipped ones on carved statues, only his were so warm and soft. She dented in his lower lip with her finger. "I want to kiss you, Mark, even if it's not for long, even if we have to be careful and not get carried away."

He closed his eyes as she traced the outline of his mouth.

"Could we?" she asked, lifting her finger away.

He opened his eyes again. "I guess..." He swallowed. "I guess we could count off seconds in our heads."

"You mean like when we were kids playing hide-and-seek?" She smiled.

"Yeah, like that." His gaze became heavy-lidded and filled with dark passions.

"So how did you do it you were a kid?"

"Not very well until I was about fourteen, and then I got better. I discovered what to do with my tongue."

Oh, boy. "I meant, how did you count?" Her breathing quickened at the delicious prospect ahead. "Did you say Mississippi-One, Mississippi-Two? Or One-Hundred-One, One-Hundred-Two?"

"We did the Mississippi thing." He drew her closer. "How about you?"

"We used Mississippi." She closed her eyes as his breath touched her mouth. "How many should we do it for?"

"Three," he murmured.

"Four."

"Five," he said. "Start counting."

Velvet lips settled over hers. *Mississippi-One.* Her heart went crazy. This was so good. He tasted like hot sex. *Mississippi-Two.* She pulled him closer, opened her mouth. *Mississippi-Three.* The warm stroke of his tongue made her whimper. *Mississippi....* She lost track as he took command. *Mississi—oh, yes. Like that. Exactly like—*

He pulled away, gasping. Then he cupped her head and cradled it against his chest as he swayed to the music. His chest continued to heave as he bowed his head over hers. "That was...a close call."

She nodded, dazed by the sexual pull of their kiss. Her whole body hummed, and tension settled between her thighs with such fierce determination that she sucked in a breath. Closing her eyes, she nestled her head against the soft silk of his dress shirt while she struggled with her urges. His heart beat wildly under her ear. Finally she cleared the huskiness from her throat. "I forgot to count."

His chest began to shake, and she finally realized he was laughing in between gasps.

His voice rasped in her ear. "No kidding."

Still shocked by the power of that brief kiss, she raised her head and looked into his eyes. She'd thought it would be exciting to make love to him tonight. She hadn't expected it to become a matter of such extreme urgency that she couldn't deal with not having him. Her voice trembled. "I suppose...I suppose you usually get that kind of charge from kissing."

He shook his head. "No."

"I thought I was in the space shuttle or something."

"We sure had ignition."

"Mark, this is serious stuff here." She clutched the back of his neck in both hands. "It's like sitting on a keg of dynamite."

His dark gaze held hers. "Or a nuclear bomb."

"Yeah." She cleared her throat again. "Here's the deal." She paused and took another breath. "I have to be honest with you. If you go back to Houston without making love to me, I'll be a basket case until you come back and finish what you just started."

He looked genuinely troubled. "It can't be until next weekend."

"Next *weekend?* Really? Oh, Mark."

"I know, but next week's packed for me."

"For me, too," she said with a soft groan. "I have two hiking trips, back-to-back." Her pulse was still racing. All thoughts of cleverly seducing him were gone. She spoke straight from the heart. "If you leave me this frustrated, I'm afraid I'll be a danger to myself and others out there in the wilderness."

He blinked. "God, I didn't even consider that. If I spent next week all tied up in knots because I wanted you so much, I could screw up somebody's whole portfolio. I could destroy their retirement account and trash their life's savings."

"And what about driving? We could have a wreck."

"We could step out in front of a bus."

"Well, you could. There won't be any buses on the trail. But I could fall over a cliff."

His arms tightened around her. "That's not going to happen."

"It's not?"

"No."

Her heart beat crazily. "You'll take care of this?"

"Yes." His gaze burned into hers.

She could barely breathe. "What about Ashley and Sam?"

He gazed across the dance floor. "I don't think we'll have a problem there. Take a look."

She followed the direction of his gaze and saw Sam and Ashley plastered together on the dance floor. "Wow. I guess that turned out okay."

"They wouldn't notice if we left."

She looked into his eyes and began to quiver with anticipation. "Shall we go now?"

His grip on her tightened. "Tell you what. You head on over to the elevators and I'll meet you there."

She hated to let him out of her sight. "Why aren't you going with me?"

"First I'm going to bribe the band to play another slow number right on the heels of this one, so Sam and Ashley will stay occupied and not miss us. Then I'm going to the desk and get another room. One Sam doesn't have a key for."

THE MANEUVER in the lounge was easier than Mark expected. The band cooperated beautifully. Two other couples besides Sam and Ashley stayed locked together on the floor, so Mark decided he'd done everybody a good turn.

Then, heart pounding, he headed for the front desk of the hotel and spoke to the young woman behind the polished wooden counter. "I'd like a room, please."

"Do you have a reservation?" she asked.

"No. I mean, yes. I already have a room here, but I'd like another room."

"The room you have isn't acceptable?"

"The room I have is fine, but I'd like a second room." This was starting to sound like a Three Stooges routine.

The clerk looked confused, but she obediently turned to her computer. "I'll see what I can do. Name, please?"

"Mark O'Grady."

"All right, Mr. O'Grady. I see your reservation here for a double for tonight only. Do you want the other room to be for one night only, as well?"

"Yes." This was taking longer than he'd planned. He didn't like the idea of Charlie loitering beside the elevator in that dress. Somebody could get the wrong idea.

The clerk typed some more, frowned, and typed in something else. "Ah. Good. I have a room that adjoins yours. If you like, I can put it on the same bill as the—"

"No!" He paused and cleared his throat. "I really don't want an adjoining room. That is, I'd actually like a room on a different floor."

The clerk glanced at him. "You want two rooms, on different floors."

"That's right."

She typed something into her computer. "All right, Mr. O'Grady. I can accommodate that request. Another double?"

Mark felt the color rising to his face. "Actually, no. I'd like this to be a king. No, wait. What's the best room you have in the hotel?"

"The Presidential Suite, but that's quite a bit more ex—"

"I'll take it. If you have it available, that is."

"Well, yes, I do." She seemed to be trying to hide her astonishment. "Would you like that on the same credit card as the double room?"

"Yes."

"And you're sure you don't want to know what the rate is?"

"I don't care what it is." *Condoms. He didn't have any. He'd deliberately not brought them, to help keep him honest.*

"How many keys will you be needing?"

"Two," he said. Then he glanced over at the gift shop. Closed. There might be a dispenser in the men's room, but to get there he'd have to go past the lounge, and that was dangerous. He could only think of one option, and he didn't like it.

"Here you go, sir." The clerk pushed a key folder toward him. "Take the elevator all the way to the top floor. It's the door on your right as you exit the elevator. Enjoy your stay."

"Thank you. Uh, I noticed the gift shop is closed."

"Yes, sir, it closes at ten."

He wondered how in the world to ask her for what he needed. He wasn't even sure if she could provide them. "The thing is, something unexpected has come up." He gulped. Wrong choice of words. "I mean, I didn't anticipate that I would be... I was wondering...that is, I..."

She gazed at him, stone-faced. Then her expression softened and she gave him a little smile. "Just a minute, sir. I think I can help you. I'll be right back." She turned and walked into the office right behind the reservation desk.

He had no idea if she knew what he was after, although from the look on her face, he thought she'd guessed. Shifting his weight nervously, he glanced in the direction of the elevators, but he couldn't see them from here. Charlie might think he wasn't going to show up. God, he hoped she didn't go back to the lounge looking for him.

Then he heard voices coming from the office.

A man laughed. "I still say you oughta charge him for those," he said.

Then the clerk said something he couldn't quite hear, except for the words *Presidential Suite.*

"Even more reason," said the man.

The clerk, her face pink, returned with a small paper sack. "I think this is what you were looking for." She handed him the sack.

He peeked inside and, sure enough, three little foil packets lay there. He glanced up at the clerk, certain that his own cheeks were red. "Listen, I don't know where you got these, but I'll be glad to pay for—"

"Never mind." She smiled again. "Consider it my contribution to safe sex."

"Thanks." And now at least two members of the staff knew what was going on in the Presidential Suite tonight, he thought as he hurried toward the elevators. But that was okay. Just so Sam didn't know. At least not yet.

Once Sam realized they were both gone he'd figure out what they'd done, of course. Mark would have to face the music in the morning.

And he knew Sam wouldn't be happy. But when Mark explained that he had to do this to keep Charlie from falling off a cliff, Sam would understand. Besides, considering the way Sam had been holding onto Ashley the last time Mark had checked, Sam might be very mellow by tomorrow morning.

As SHE STOOD by the elevator waiting for Mark, Charlie opened her tiny red purse and took out her lipstick. The brass elevator doors made a reasonable mirror, but her hands were shaking so much she had a tough time getting the lipstick on straight.

Well, she'd done it. She'd convinced him to throw caution to the winds and make love. And now she was scared silly.

So much depended on this encounter. After all, both of them had been quite open in their letters about wanting to find a mate. And no matter how attracted they were to each other, if the sex turned out to be a disaster, they might decide to end the relationship tonight.

Now that the moment was at hand, she was afraid she'd misrepresented herself to him and he'd be disappointed. She'd billed herself as a sexually adventurous woman because she'd wanted to attract a sexually adventurous man.

Mark had sounded that way in his letters, too, but he'd turned out to be a bit more conservative in person, considering his hesitation in the beginning. Was he expecting her to be the aggressor once they were alone?

While writing to him in the privacy of her apartment, she'd been so sure that she could be that kind of woman. She sought out adventure in her work, why not in her sexual relationships? Now she wasn't so confident. She tucked her lipstick back in her purse, right next to the two condoms she'd brought along, just in case. Well, just in case was about to happen, exactly as she'd fantasized.

She was about to discover whether she had the nerve to turn fantasy into reality. Fluffing her short hair with her fingers, she gazed at her reflection. She certainly looked the part. It was quite a dress. No wonder Ashley had been worried.

A couple approached the elevators. Although they pretended not to notice her, Charlie knew better. While they waited for the elevator they kept glancing in the polished brass doors to check her out.

It didn't take much imagination to guess what they were thinking. Any woman loitering by the elevator at this hour, in this outfit, had to be waiting for the man of the evening to get a room for the two of them. Not many other explanations came to mind. After what seemed like eons, the elevator arrived and whisked the couple away.

More eons seemed to pass as she paced the area pretending to study the potted philodendron, the blinking lights above the elevator, and the hotel's insignia stamped into the sand of the ashtray.

"Charlie. Here I am. I'm so sorry to keep you waiting."

She turned, her heart racing, to find Mark coming toward her. Well, this was it. Warmth flooded through her. He *was* a very yummy-looking guy. Maybe she could be more aggressive than she'd thought.

He'd hooked his jacket over his shoulder and he held a key folder in his free hand. He smiled at her, looking far more confident than she felt. "I thought I'd be faster."

"It's okay." She was impressed that he'd remembered to grab his jacket from the back of his chair. "Sam and Ashley didn't see you?"

"Nope. They were very involved." He tucked the key folder in his jacket pocket and looped the jacket over one arm before stepping over to the elevator and punching the button. His finger trembled the slightest little bit. Maybe he wasn't totally cool about this, either.

"I'm glad it seems to be working out for them," she said.

"Me, too. For several reasons." He cleared his throat and glanced at her. For the first time since he'd approached the elevator he looked unsure of himself. "By the way, I don't want you to worry about...well, anything. That is, I have..."

"Oh." She blushed. "I have some, too."

"Yeah?"

His look of surprise made her feel the need to explain. "It's probably my backpacking experience. When you're heading into the wilderness, you try to anticipate every—"

He stepped toward her and cupped her warm cheek in his hand. "I think it's wonderful that you brought condoms," he murmured, gazing into her eyes. "I'm flattered that you brought them, to tell the truth. I should have, but I'd really decided this wasn't going to happen."

When he stood this close to her she had trouble breathing. But she wanted to say something important, so she drew in a quick breath and used it all in one rushed little speech. "In our letters, we talked a lot about how great sex would be between us, but what if it's not?"

There. She'd put her worst fear out where they could see it. She gasped for air and searched his gaze as she waited for his response.

He rubbed his thumb over her cheek in a lazy caress and his confident manner returned. "That's never crossed my mind."

"It hasn't?" She peered at him in astonishment. "Why not?"

He looked genuinely puzzled. "Why would it?"

"Well, because we've never been together, and everybody has different reactions to...I mean, not everyone has the same..." She stared at him as he continued to look bewildered. "You've never had bad sex?" she asked finally.

"No. No, I haven't." He sounded surprised that she'd even ask. "Why, have you?"

"Of *course*. I thought everyone had."

"Not me. I don't understand how you could. I mean, everything about it is so wonderful. It doesn't matter if you're cramped, or the temperature's not right, or you don't have a lot of time. It's still..." His eyes glowed as he gazed into hers. "Making love is great," he finished softly. "And this will be the best."

She was totally astounded. Everyone she'd ever known who was willing to talk about it had been able to come up with at least one horror story.

"The elevator's here." He stroked her cheek one last time and moved his hand to the small of her back. "Let's go," he murmured.

She stepped into the mirror and wood-paneled cubicle ahead of him. "You really never have had a bad time of it?" she asked again as she turned to face him.

"No, I really never have," he said with a patient smile. "Women are designed for such pleasure, how could you end up with anything else?"

"Now I'm really intimidated. I could be your first catastrophe."

"Not possible." He punched the button for their floor.

"Of course it's possible."

"Nope. And I'll show you why." He handed her his coat. "Would you hold this a minute?"

"Okay." She wasn't sure what was going on, but she took the coat.

"This is why." He cradled her face in both hands and covered her mouth with his.

And there it was again—Fourth of July going on inside her body. Oh, that mouth, that tongue.... Her thighs began to tremble and her heartbeat pounded in her ears. She'd never been this pumped up, not even when she was about to run Class Five rapids.

He lifted his mouth a fraction from hers. "That's why," he whispered. "I've had good sex with every woman I've made love to, and none of their kisses felt as exciting as yours, so how can we go wrong?"

She couldn't talk. She could only moan a little. Apparently she'd stumbled onto a man who was an artist when it came to making love, and tonight he planned to create a masterpiece. Who was she to argue with that?

6

IF MARK HAD BEEN having second thoughts about the wisdom of making love to Charlie tonight, those second thoughts disintegrated the moment he kissed her again. As he'd thought the first time, she tasted and felt like his forever girl. Everything about her was right, from the spicy scent of her perfume to the shape of her mouth, from the color of her eyes to the way her body fit against his.

He'd always loved sex in general, and that had been part of his problem. He'd taken such pleasure in good sex that he hadn't considered even greater sex awaited him with the right woman, the perfect woman: Charlie.

Apparently she'd had some bad experiences with lovemaking. He shouldn't have been surprised. Come to think of it, all the women he'd made love to had told him of bad experiences. That had been another one of his problems, wanting to make it up to them for the crummy lovers they'd been with before. Obviously he'd been successful, too, because each of his fiancées had raved about the good times they'd had in bed with him.

But difficult as it was for him to admit, sex wasn't everything. At some point you had to climb out of bed and live together. He and his fiancées hadn't had enough in common to do that. But he and Charlie did. They'd discussed it all in their letters.

For three months they'd been building toward what was about to happen between them tonight. Their communication had created a tsunami wave of urges, and it was about to crash onto the shore. Sensible behavior was a joke in a situation like this. To deny the power of their attraction, to put it off until another time, was going against the laws of nature.

He had no intention of running from his destiny.

The elevator slid open on the top floor. No one had interrupted their elevator ride, and he took that as a good sign. "We're here," he said, looking into her passion-glazed eyes.

Her voice was husky with desire. "Good."

"Come on." Wrapping an arm around her waist, he guided her out of the elevator and turned to the right, as the clerk had directed him. At the end of the hall was a set of double doors. The number on the brass plate beside the door matched the number on his key folder. He'd never stayed in the Presidential Suite of any hotel before, but no time could be more fitting than this.

As they walked toward the double doors, Charlie drew in a quick breath. "Mark, this looks pretty fancy. What kind of room did you get?"

"The right kind."

"But we didn't really need—"

"Yes, we did. Remember how we talked about letting go for a big splurge, even when your day-to-day living is more conservative?"

"Well, yes, but I still think—"

"Charlie, let yourself enjoy this. Let yourself pretend for one night that we're jet-setters. Maybe next weekend we'll go camping and rough it. But we can have fun with both, right?"

She gazed up at him. "You do know me."

"I think I do." He gave her a quick squeeze. "I need my jacket back. The keys are in the pocket." So were the three condoms the desk clerk had given him. He'd ditched the paper sack. He'd appreciated her delicacy in disguising what she was handing to him, but no way was he riding up the elevator to the Presidential Suite holding condoms in a paper sack. Jet-setters didn't do that.

Charlie handed him his coat. He didn't want to let go of her for even a minute, but he needed two hands to get the key out of the key folder in his pocket. Even so he fumbled once before he finally stuck the key in the lock and opened the door into a foyer.

Charlie gasped again. "Oh, Mark. This is...amazing."

"I think it's about right." He guided her into the entryway and his feet sank into thick carpet. A huge vase of flowers sat on a table in front of a large oval mirror, and soft music played somewhere in the interior of the suite.

"Look at these flowers," she said.

"I'm looking at you." His breathing quickened and he wanted her so much he felt dizzy. If he reached for her now, they'd make love right here on the floor.

But he thought they should absorb the ambiance of the place first. Tonight would be a very significant memory for both of them, and now that they were alone, he didn't want to rush it.

He smiled at her. "Go on in and look around. I'll lock up."

"All right," she said with an answering smile.

Closing the door and flipping the dead bolt, he took the time to transfer the condoms to his pants pocket before following Charlie down the short hallway.

In the doorway to the main part of the suite, she

glanced over her shoulder at him. "I'll bet this is the best room in the entire hotel, isn't it?"

"Yep." He grinned, congratulating himself on making this choice. "I'm glad it was available."

"Well, so am I, because it's gorgeous. But you don't need to go making this a habit. I like simple things, too." She walked into the main room.

"I know." He leaned in the doorway and felt very proud of himself as he watched her. "I was listening, Charlie. For three months I've been listening. I know your favorite flowers are daisies. If I'd had more notice that we'd be here, I'd have filled the rooms with daisies."

She turned to gaze at him. "Don't even think of apologizing. I've never stayed in a place like this before. Not that I'm exactly *staying* here, of course."

"Yes, you are. You're staying here with me." He sure liked the sound of that.

"This is really stupendous." She spun in a slow circle. "You could have a party for fifty people in here."

"Let's not," he said as he surveyed the setting he'd chosen for his Charlie.

The lighting was subdued and elegant, the color scheme ivory and gold. The furniture looked antique, except perhaps for the longest sofa he'd ever seen in his life. He couldn't help thinking about what might be done with a sofa that big and luxurious.

Another huge vase of flowers sat on the coffee table, and a full-size dining table and eight chairs stood over by the floor-to-ceiling windows. The lights of the city shone through the sheer drapes covering the windows.

"No, let's not invite anyone but us," she agreed softly. "Two is the perfect number."

"I'm partial to that number, myself." He loved the

sound of her voice. He'd begun to yearn for her even more after the first time he heard it on the telephone about three weeks ago. But hearing her voice on the phone didn't compare to listening in person and watching her lips move as she formed each word. He was mesmerized by her lips. He wanted to feel them over every inch of his body.

"Mark, I can't believe you rented this fabulous suite for our first night together. You make me feel so special."

He gazed at her standing in the middle of the ivory-and-gold room in her red, sexy dress, her color high, her eyes sparkling. "You *are* special," he said. "And the suite is nothing. But looking at you, knowing that we're finally alone—now that's about as special as it gets."

Her cheeks turned even pinker as she gestured to the doorway of the bedroom. "Shall we...see what the rest is like?"

"Absolutely." The rest was what interested him most. And when she started walking toward the bedroom, he knew exactly how he wanted this to start out. "Wait."

She turned back, a question in her eyes.

"I want to carry you through that doorway."

From the brilliance of her answering smile, he knew his instincts were right on. Tossing his coat on the long ivory sofa, he crossed the room and lifted her into his arms. Damn, but she felt good there.

She wrapped her arms around his neck and looked deep into his eyes. "It's as if you've set out to make all my dreams come true."

"I hope I can, because you're my dream come true." Heart pounding with anticipation, he carried her over the threshold.

Oh, yes, this room was the right choice. What a contrast with the one he was renting for him and Sam, with its typical quilted bedspreads covering a bed connected to a built-in headboard. Standard fare.

Not here. The dark antique furniture gleamed and gave a sense of permanence and tradition to the room. Mark wanted to create traditions with Charlie. They both loved holidays, and dogs, and lazy Sunday mornings. He laid her gently on a canopied bed covered in yards of white lace.

Her voice trembled. "Oh, Mark."

He leaned closer. "I'm here. Right here." He closed his eyes, almost tasting the kiss that would soon be his.

The bedside phone jangled.

He opened his eyes and looked into hers as the phone rang again. They both turned their heads and looked at it. In keeping with the decor, the phone was a tasteful white-and-gold reproduction of an antique. That didn't make the noise it was giving out any more appealing to Mark.

"You know who it is," Charlie said.

"Yep."

"Maybe you should answer it, so they know we're okay."

He continued to stare at the ringing telephone, willing it to shut up. "Are you sure?"

"Yes."

With a sigh he reached over and picked up the delicate receiver. "Hello, Sam."

"Where the hell are you?" Sam's voice was tight with fury.

"I'm afraid I can't tell you that, but all is well."

"The hell it is. Damn it, Mark. I thought we had an agreement."

"And I'd planned to stick by it, but that was before I kissed Charlie." He glanced over at her and smiled. "That changed everything."

"You're hopeless, you know that? Totally hopeless!" Sam sounded terminally disgusted with him. "You're gonna make love to that woman, aren't you?"

Mark continued to gaze into Charlie's eyes. "Looks like it."

Sam let out a heavy sigh of frustration. "I shoulda known you'd end up like this the minute I saw that red dress."

Charlie snuggled closer to Mark. "Ask him if he'd please take Ashley home, okay?"

Mark nodded. "Listen, Sam, Charlie wants to know if you'd take Ashley home."

"What if I refuse to do that unless you get your sorry ass down here?"

"I'm not coming down, and you're too much of a gentleman to leave Ashley in the lurch."

Sam blew out another breath. "I can't *believe* you did this. Well, yes, I can, but I don't want to. I want to wring your neck, but it seems I can't find out where you are without knocking on every damned door in the hotel, and I'd probably be arrested before I found the right one."

"Just give it up, Sam."

But Sam had more to say on the subject. "I hope you know you confused the hell out of the poor desk clerk. But, of course, like most women, she's fallen prey to your charms. I tried to bribe her to give me your room number, but she wouldn't."

"That has nothing to do with my charms. She'd lose her job if she gave out the room number."

Charlie smoothed her finger over his lower lip and smiled. "No, it's your charm."

"It's your charm," Sam echoed. "I told her I was a doctor and you were my brother and that it was up to me to give you your medication. All she'd let me do is call you on the house phone."

Mark chuckled. "Listen, I gotta go. Thanks for taking care of Ashley, buddy."

"Don't you *buddy* me. I just have one thing to say to you. If it's not too late already, don't you dare propose to her!"

Mark ignored that as he looked at Charlie. "Do you have any other messages for Sam?"

"Just ask him to tell Ashley that I'm fine, and I'll see her in the morning."

As Mark relayed the request he realized Charlie was unbuttoning his shirt.

"She won't be fine if you propose to her and then back out!" Sam bellowed. "If I can't stop you from doing the deed, at least don't propose to her!"

Charlie was pretty good at this button business. Soon she'd unfastened enough that she could pull apart his shirt and press her lips against his chest. He began to wonder what he was doing holding a telephone receiver to his ear when he could be doing much more interesting things.

"I think we've covered everything, Sam," he said. "I'll see you in the coffee shop tomorrow morning around ten, okay?"

"Don't *propose!*" Sam shouted.

"Good night, Sam."

As Charlie began to lick his nipples, he groaned and tried to put the receiver back in its cradle. It took three tries, and all the while he could hear Sam shouting at him.

"What's he saying?" Charlie murmured, her breath warm against his skin as she nibbled and licked his bare chest.

"I have absolutely no idea." Mark let go of the receiver and abandoned himself to the joy of her moist kisses.

BREATHING IN THE SCENT of Mark's skin, Charlie felt like a kitten with her first taste of cream. The more she used her tongue to explore and excite him, the more she wanted to use it. He was delicious. Talk about a chemistry lesson. She'd never had this kind of basic hunger for a man's body in her life. She couldn't get his clothes off fast enough.

And then he interfered with her progress by grasping both hands right when she'd nearly unfastened his slacks. "Wait," he murmured.

"I want—"

"And I want you to." He rolled her onto her back, pressing her against the lace and satin coverlet as he kissed both her hands. "Soon. Not yet."

The coverlet under her bare back felt like a giant wedding ring pillow. She thought about that, and then Mark slipped his hand inside her dress and she couldn't think anymore.

Gazing into her eyes, he slowly stroked her breast. "Remember telling me how sensitive you are here?"

She trembled under the practiced touch of his hand. "Yes," she whispered. But she had never been this sensitive. And no man had ever caressed her this way, looking deep into her eyes while he touched her with infinite gentleness, infinite care. For the first time in her life she felt cherished by a lover.

"When you put on this dress, did you imagine me doing this?"

She nodded. But her imagination had failed her. She'd imagined him pulling the dress away in a frenzy of lust. This slow seduction, this building of anticipation for what was to come, was so much more exciting that she was shaking.

With a smooth movement of his hand, he stroked upward and pushed the dress off her shoulder. Still he held her gaze, postponing the moment when he would look at her. Heat shimmered in his eyes. "Did you imagine me undressing you?"

"Yes." She swallowed. "But I thought it would be fast."

"Did you?" He eased the dress off her other shoulder. "Even after you told me in a letter that you would like it to be slow and easy, to draw out the anticipation?"

"I thought..." She had trouble breathing. "I thought...that would happen later. I thought that the first time you wouldn't be able to go slow."

"When it comes to loving you, I can do anything." He feathered a kiss over her lips. "Anything at all." Then he kissed her in earnest, making her mind spin and her body moisten while he slowly, carefully drew the top of her dress down to her waist.

He lifted his mouth a fraction. "Now lie still," he murmured. "Now that I can finally see your breasts, I want to take my time looking." There was a smile in his voice. "This is to satisfy the voyeur in me, and the tiny bit of exhibitionist in you."

"I'm not an—"

"Yes, you are. A tiny bit. Or you'd never have worn that dress. And I love that you wanted to show off for me. I hope you'll do it again. But I want my reward for being teased in the restaurant and on the dance floor. So don't rush me, Charlie."

She shivered with pleasure. He really had seen into the depths of her soul. She'd tested herself in other areas of her life, but never this way, and he knew she longed to push the envelope here, too. No wonder he'd never had a bad experience in bed with a woman. He paid attention, and he had perfect instincts.

Slowly he pushed himself to a sitting position and his gaze moved from her face to her breasts. He exhaled a deep breath. "Oh, Charlie. You were worth waiting for."

Her nipples tingled and tightened as he continued to look.

"You're so perfect," he said softly. "I love that tiny freckle beside your nipple."

She'd never been studied with such care, as if he were memorizing her and stroking her with his glance. A warm flush of arousal spread over her skin.

"You like me to look at you like this," he said, "don't you?"

"Can...can you tell?"

"Yes. By the way your nipples have darkened. They're so taut and ready. And your breasts are so rosy."

She moaned. "Oh, please. Please...kiss me there."

He leaned over her, the hair on his chest tickling her throbbing nipples. "I will." He nibbled at her mouth, her chin, her earlobes. "I will kiss you everywhere, Charlie. Even the places you think you're too shy for."

Her heart raced. So he remembered that, too. She'd

confided that, although she was sexually adventurous, it might have to be coaxed out of her. He'd promised to make her feel uninhibited. The letters they'd written in those last few days had nearly scorched her hands as she'd read them.

"I had no appetite for dinner." His tongue found the hollow of her throat. "But I'm dying of hunger for you."

"Love me, Mark. I've waited so long." *All her life.* She tunneled her fingers in his hair, cupping his head as he trailed kisses along her collarbone and down the slope of her breast. When his mouth finally closed over her nipple, she cried out with pleasure.

Yet that was only the beginning. All God's creatures had a special talent, and she was learning Mark's. Somehow he knew...everything—when to move fast, when to slow down. When to lick and when to nibble. And where. Lord, did he know where.

She'd never known the underside of her breasts was an erogenous zone, or the spot right below her ribs, or her navel. By the time he'd dipped his tongue into that small hollow, she was a churning mass of needs, a shameless wanton who was so eager that, when he slipped both hands under her, she lifted away from the mattress so he could pull down the zipper of her dress.

"Ah, Charlie. I'll bet you want to show off those black panties for me."

"I do," she said breathlessly. But as he peeled her dress down, she realized she was still wearing her red high-heeled sandals. "My shoes—"

"Are staying on." His voice was gruff with passion. "That's for the slightly kinky streak we both have." He worked the dress over her feet, and his breath caught. "Oh, yeah. Black lace and red heels."

She quivered as he lifted her foot to run his tongue

along her arch. Then he kissed the inside of her ankle and licked his way with maddening slowness up her quivering calf, all the while coaxing her legs farther apart.

"Feeling brave?" he murmured. Without waiting for an answer, he bent her leg and pressed his mouth against the back of her knee. Once he'd firmly established that she loved being kissed there by making her moan and writhe on the bed, he began a lazy journey up her inner thigh.

She clutched the coverlet and struggled for breath. "The lights," she said as an attack of modesty struck. "I wish you'd turn off—"

"Nope."

"But—"

His warm breath reminded her exactly where he was, hovering over the elastic of her panties. Tiny kisses punctuated his words. "You told me you might need to be pushed a little."

"I don't remember." But she did. She'd been so daring on paper.

"I do. And I'm pushing." His tongue traced the ridge of elastic circling her thigh. "Let me love you, Charlie, with the lights on."

Her heart had never beat so fast in her life, not even when she'd hung over a hundred-foot chasm on the end of a rope. "I'm sort of...scared."

He nipped the elastic with his teeth. "And sort of excited?"

Her throat felt tight. "Yes."

"Be patient, Charlie." His lingering kisses moved up the side seam of her panties and across the bikini-line top. "In a few seconds you won't be scared at all."

She lay there trembling uncontrollably. Her view of

the white canopy over her head blurred as he moved lower, his lips brushing the lace, his tongue tracing its pattern. At last he pressed his mouth against the wet material covering his ultimate destination. The heat of his mouth and the firm pressure shot straight through to her womb and she gasped.

He breathed in. "Mmm. So sweet." He nuzzled her through the thin layer of satin.

Oh, that was good. Oh, that was *very* good. Her limbs grew heavy as a warm, syrupy feeling slipped through her body. And a wonderful tingling, tightening sensation swirled right *there*. Oh, yes. More of that. More...

And then, with casual ease, he pulled the material aside, leaving nothing between her and his hot, seeking tongue. No defenses. No fear. No restraint. Free-fall. Soft cries spilled from her lips as he coaxed her toward surrender.

And when her climax arrived, her response tumbled around them. Wild with the joy of it, she arched into his liquid caress and called his name, over and over, until she collapsed back upon the coverlet, eyes closed, breath coming in ragged spurts.

Gently he drew her panties off, and she could barely summon the strength to help him.

"You've...turned me into a rag doll," she murmured, so warm and contented as she watched him leave the bed and begin removing the rest of his clothes.

His glance swept over her. "A rag doll in red shoes. I couldn't ask for more."

"But I won't...be any fun."

"Sure you will," he said softly as he tossed his shirt across a nearby wing chair. "Give yourself a little time to recover, and you'll be dynamite." He kicked off his shoes and made short work of his socks.

"I may never recover." She gazed at him while he took off his slacks. Then he shoved down his briefs. "Then again...."

His smile was slow and easy, the smile of a man who knew what to do with the generous gift he'd been given. "You're recovering already." He levered himself onto the mattress.

She couldn't believe how the sight of his erect penis affected her. He'd just given her a shattering orgasm, and yet she was beginning to ache all over again. "Now look who's beautiful," she murmured, sliding her hand down the velvet length of his shaft.

"And holding on by a thread," he said in a thick voice.

"But I want to touch you." She wrapped her fingers around that tempting toy. "I want to—"

"Don't I wish," he said, gasping as he carefully removed her hand. He turned toward the bedside table and picked up a foil-wrapped condom. "I thought maybe we could fool around a little, but not this time. My control's shot."

She wasn't about to argue with him. The hollowness within her begged for what he had to give. She grew moist and ready just watching him roll the condom on.

He finished putting it on and glanced at her. "Maybe it's the shoes. I'm going crazy wanting to make love to you, knowing you're still wearing those sexy shoes."

She felt a quick stab of fear. The shoes were nothing like she usually wore. Tonight she'd gone for the glamour look, but she'd never be able to keep up that image on a regular basis. She smiled, to make her comment sound like a joke. "So you'd lose interest if I happened to be barefoot?"

He laughed and pulled her into his arms. "Not a chance."

"Usually I wear running shoes."

He nuzzled her neck. "While you're making love?"

"No." She was losing her train of thought. He was so good, so very good at this. "I mean... I'm not the high-heel type. I'm the running-shoes type."

He eased her to her back and his voice was soft as he moved between her thighs. "Please don't run away from me, Charlie."

She looked up into his brown eyes, so filled with desire for her. *Oh, please let this be real.* "I'm not running."

"Neither am I." He probed gently, then slid deep with a satisfied groan. "Oh, Charlie." His voice caught. "I belong here."

"Yes." She held on tight, afraid to move. A feeling this perfect didn't come along every day. Being completely united with Mark was like having every good moment in her life distilled into one pure drop of happiness. He was an ice cream cone on a hot day, a campfire on a chilly night, wildflowers in the spring and pumpkins in October.

Staying perfectly still and locked tight within her, he searched her gaze with his. "Maybe it was only letters." He combed his fingers tenderly through her hair. "But my heart was in those letters."

She swallowed. "Mine, too."

"But still I signed them *Cheers,* or *Take Care.*"

She had, too, been careful. So careful.

"I wanted to write *Love, Mark.*"

Her heart swelled with an almost painful happiness. "You did?"

He nodded, and his voice grew husky. "I love you,

Charlie. Even before tonight, I've loved you. I knew you'd be like this, so warm and beautiful and *right*."

Her throat tightened with emotion as she trembled on the brink of tears. If he could dare such a statement, so could she. After all, it was the truth. She'd fallen more in love with him with each letter, even though she'd never been bold enough to sign hers that way, either, even though she'd been afraid of getting hurt.

She gazed into his eyes. "I love you, too."

He closed his eyes. "Thank God." When he opened them again, his eyes were luminous. "Then you don't think I'm crazy."

"No. Not unless we both are."

"Then be crazy with me." He began to move within her. "Be crazy in love with me."

All her doubts evaporated in the heat of his loving. They moved together as if they'd been born to bring each other pleasure. But soon even the word *pleasure* was too tame for the forces building within her.

Wild and unrestrained, her response dwarfed that first spike of temporary excitement he'd given her at first. Wonderful though it had been, it seemed minor now—an amusement park water slide compared to a plunge through raging currents as they headed for a thundering waterfall. With each powerful thrust he brought them closer to the edge.

"Be with me," he whispered urgently.

"*Yes.*" The waterfall pounded in her ears. Her body rose and fell with the turbulence of their mating.

"Be with me always."

"Oh, yes. *Yes.*" Her cries blended with his as she tumbled over with him, both of them hurtling toward a cataclysmic release. And through it all she held onto him for dear life. For life.

Afterward they lay sprawled together on the coverlet, both of them gasping for breath.

Finally Mark dragged himself up on one elbow and gazed down at her. "So it's settled, then. We're getting married."

She smiled at him through tears of happiness. "Of course we are."

7

SAM SPEWED HIS COFFEE halfway across the table. "You did *what?*"

"Take it easy, okay?" Mark glanced around at the other customers in the hotel coffee shop. "People are staring."

"That's because they've probably never seen a bigger idiot in their lives! Make that two. I'm an even bigger one than you for imagining for a minute that this might not happen. Of course it was going to happen, because you are doomed to—"

"Sam, she's the one. This is it."

Sam began mopping up the table. "Now there's an original line. Let me see. Have I ever heard that one before? Oh, come to think of it, I have. Only about *five times.* Dear Lord in heaven."

Mark had expected this reaction. He'd called wolf too many times. But Sam had to understand this time was for real. He leaned closer. "I swear to you, it's true. I'll swear on anything you want. My Astros season tickets. If I screw this up, you can have mine and give them to whoever you want sitting next to you this season."

"If you screw this up, you won't dare appear in public, so you might as well hand over those tickets, and the Oilers tickets, while you're at it."

"Sam, I'll put anything you want on the line. My car, my DVD player, my CD collection, my pool cue."

"Your pool cue?" Sam glanced up from his mopping. "Now that would make things interesting. I've always coveted that pool cue. But don't be giving me your Billy Bass. I don't want a singing fish."

"You're trying to make a joke out of this, but I'm not kidding. What can I do to convince you I'm sincere?"

"Oh, I believe you're sincere." Sam tossed his soggy napkin on the plate and grabbed a fresh one to blot the coffee from his mustache.

"Then what's the problem?"

Sam looked extremely weary. "Just because you believe all this now doesn't mean you'll believe it later. You're sincere as hell until you figure out that good sex doesn't make up for a tendency to nag, or to gossip endlessly on the cell phone, or to run up the credit cards buying expensive clothes, or to hate hiking and camping, or to be a terminally boring conversationalist. Have I covered all the fatal flaws that have dynamited your impending nuptials?"

"That's just it." Mark grew desperate to convince Sam that this time was different. "Charlie doesn't have any of those flaws. We've been through it all in the letters. We really are compatible, Sam. The whole *Texas Men* magazine idea of yours worked like a charm."

"Letters aren't enough." Sam pushed away his plate and leaned back in the booth. "As I've said about a million times, you have to spend time with her, and time spent doing the hootchie-coo doesn't count. You never notice a woman's flaws during those moments, because you're so in love with the whole concept of sex. One of *your* biggest flaws is that you're too damned good in bed. It's a real failing."

Mark laughed. Despite the seriousness of the moment, he couldn't help it. Nobody had ever accused him of being too good in bed. "Failing?"

"Yes, failing! Women sense your inborn talent and flock to you as a result. You naturally accommodate them, and you do it so well that neither one of you is left with a brain cell working. You're every woman's fantasy in the beginning, but before the sad story plays out, you're every woman's nightmare."

"Not Charlie's. I won't be Charlie's nightmare. We're perfect for each other."

He sighed. "I suppose that's always possible, but I want you two to have a long, long courtship before I even think about renting a tuxedo."

"We're planning to get married in two weeks."

Sam's eyes widened. "You're kidding."

"Nope. The sooner the better. It'll be a small ceremony, so—"

"It'll be a nonexistent ceremony. We're going to fix this." He glanced at his watch. "You say she left for home about an hour ago, so she's had time to change clothes and relax a little. We'll drive over there right now and tell her you were a bit premature. Hug, hug, kiss, kiss, cancel, cancel. Come on."

"No."

Sam gave him a warning look. "Then I guess you really want Jack to be your best man."

The thought made Mark's stomach churn. "No, I want you to be my best man. But if you don't feel you can stand up with me in two weeks, then I'll ask Jack. Because I am marrying Charlie the Saturday after next."

Sam's steely gaze wavered. "You'd really ask Jack?"

"If I have to."

"And I suppose Ashley will be the maid of honor."

"That's who Charlie's planning to ask." He sensed a weak spot in Sam's armor. Judging from Sam's earlier comments, he and Ashley had gotten along great. They hadn't made as much progress as he and Charlie, but they'd become very friendly before Sam had kissed Ashley good-night at her door in the wee hours of the morning.

Mark cleared his throat. "I'm sure Jack and Ashley will enjoy each other's company," he said casually.

Sam's jaw clenched. "Oh, I wouldn't doubt that. I know Jack."

"We're planning something very simple. Just a best man for me and a maid of honor for Charlie. No other attendants. Just Charlie, me, Ashley, and...Jack, I guess. A late afternoon ceremony, followed by an intimate little dinner with family and friends, probably at the same restaurant where we ate last night, because that's where Charlie and I first met face-to-face."

"Do you hear yourself?" Sam grumbled. "You met her *last night*. And now you're planning the wedding."

"When we actually met isn't the point. We're in sync, Charlie and me. I suggested Jamaica for the honeymoon and she can hardly wait. We'll leave that next morning." He paused. "I suppose Jack will stay in Austin on Saturday night, maybe even do some sightseeing with Ashley the next day."

Sam gazed into his coffee mug. "You are such a damned pain in the ass. You know perfectly well I don't want Jack hanging around Austin."

"Then be my best man, okay? This is it—the very last time I'll ever ask you."

"Okay." Sam glanced up at him. "But I swear to God, if you back out this time, I'm going to join the DOA Support Group. I'll be a T-shirt-wearing, card-carrying member, maybe even president, and your life won't be worth living."

"I understand. It isn't going to happen." Mark remembered all the morning-after sessions with Sam when he'd announced his five other proposals. In all those other sessions he'd never felt so elated, so sure, so completely happy as he did at this moment. "Trust me."

Sam sighed and pushed his plate away. "I have no choice. I can't have you standing up there with Jack, and I especially can't have Jack standing up there with Ashley. He's not even remotely good enough for her. Now come on, let's get out of this joint."

"Fine with me." Mark was too excited to eat, anyway. "I have a bunch of things to do. Charlie and I are going camping next weekend, so that leaves me less time to take care of the details."

Sam stood. "At least you're taking her camping. That's a good sign." He sighed. "Maybe this will work out. But I'm afraid to hope. The setup is too sickeningly familiar for me to have hope."

"It will work out." Mark paid the bill and they both walked out carrying their garment bags over their shoulders.

In no time they were on the freeway bound for Houston, with Mark singing along to the radio. He felt great.

"I assume you told her about your other engagements, at least," Sam said.

"Uh, not exactly."

"Not *exactly*?" Sam reached over and switched off the radio. "What the hell does that mean?"

"I couldn't tell her right then, Sam. She was so happy, and I was so happy."

"And Mr. Happy was so happy. Lord Almighty, you are a piece of work. And when are you planning to break the news?"

"Next weekend will be perfect." He switched the radio back on, determined to maintain the good mood he was in. "We'll have plenty of time and we'll be out in the woods, enjoying nature. That's a much better time to tell her."

Sam turned the radio off again. "I'm not so sure. You'll be all alone out there. Nowhere to run if she gets homicidal."

"She won't. You really do worry too much."

"And you don't worry enough!"

"She'll be fine with it. You'll see." Mark punched the button for the radio, although his mood wasn't quite as jolly as it had been. Sam had found his only source of doubt, which was just like Sam—always looking at the horse poop instead of the pony.

But in this case, the horse poop might make a difference. Revealing his past was the only thing that scared him about this engagement. Each of the other women had known way ahead of time. They'd taken it as a challenge to try and break the curse.

He wasn't sure if Charlie would take that attitude. Therefore he wanted the setting and the mood to be just right before he told her about his miserable record with weddings. It was a touchy subject, no question.

Sam threw up his hands. "Well, maybe I won't have to worry about you running out on her. Maybe when you finally confess your sins next weekend, she'll push you over a cliff or drown you in the river. End of story."

THREE DAYS LATER, Charlie entered her apartment feeling very grubby from leading city slickers on a three-day hike through the hill country. The message light was blinking on her answering machine, and she knew some of those flashing signals were from Mark. Her darling Mark. How she missed him.

She wanted to call him back immediately, but she also hoped to spend at least an hour on the phone with him when she did. Before that she needed to stop by Glam Girl and discuss a few details of the wedding with Ashley.

Then, once she was in for the night, she could call Mark. Maybe she'd run herself a nice deep bubble bath and call him while she was in the tub. That could be fun.

After dumping off her gear, she hopped back in her dusty Miata and drove toward Ashley's shop. It was nearly five. Her timing was perfect. Maybe she and Ashley could go out for a bite to eat, since Charlie didn't think she had a thing in the house worth cooking.

Once she was married, Mark would handle the kitchen chores, and she was looking forward to that. He'd said he loved to cook, and with his sensuous nature she figured he was probably really good at it. Oh, he was sensuous, all right. They'd gotten very little sleep the rest of the night she'd spent in the suite with him. This weekend would be more of the same, except they'd be inside a tent.

Or maybe they'd try a change of scene. She fantasized making love to him in the middle of a little glen, where the wild grass grew thick enough to make a spongy carpet. Just thinking of that made her hot. She'd better direct her mind elsewhere if she expected to have a coherent conversation with Ashley.

Ashley hadn't been overjoyed with the news at first, but she'd come around. Once she'd realized Charlie was totally in love, Ashley had started believing the wedding might be a good thing. Both sisters would miss living in the same town, but Houston wasn't so far away. As an added perk, Ashley would have an excuse to spend more time with Sam.

Charlie was relieved once her sister came on board. Besides appreciating her moral support, she needed her for some practical matters. Ashley had more of a flair for wedding-related details than Charlie, and her contacts in retail would help them come up with two dresses on short notice. Fortunately, Ashley was willing to do any necessary alterations herself.

Their parents had been another tough sell, but at last they'd given their blessing and had promised to fly down for the ceremony. This weekend Mark planned to call them before he drove back to Houston, so he could start getting acquainted, at least by telephone.

She'd suggested calling his mother, too, but Mark seemed to think his mother would respond better if they told her after they were married. That was the only aspect of the wedding that bothered Charlie. She couldn't imagine any mother preferring to hear about her son's wedding after the fact. But Mark had said he'd explain all about his mother next weekend on the camping trip, when they had more time to talk.

Then he'd kissed her again, and before long she hadn't had the slightest interest in discussing his mother. But she'd thought about the situation several times since then, and she was curious. His mother lived right in Houston. Since Mark's airline pilot father had been killed in a crash ten years ago, his mother Selena was his closest family member. Not inviting her bothered Charlie more than she wanted to admit, and she hoped to change Mark's mind.

She parked diagonally in front of Glam Girl next to a

minivan. As she walked toward the shop she noticed that Ashley had several customers inside. She was happy for Ashley, who could always use the business, but she'd hoped Ashley would be finished for the day so they could talk about the wedding.

When she opened the door, her first impression was that all the women in the shop belonged to some kind of team. They wore identical T-shirts in deep purple with a logo on the front.

Ashley glanced toward the door as Charlie walked in. "Charlie, these women are here to see you. When you didn't answer your phone, they came here to find out if I knew when you'd be back."

"That's right," said a tall brunette. "We—"

"I'll give you what information I can," Charlie said, "but you'll need to make your actual reservation through the company." So they weren't Ashley's customers, but potential customers for Charlie. So much the better. With all the changes coming in her life, she could use the money.

"It's not an outdoor adventure they're after, Charlie." Ashley walked over and put an arm around her shoulders.

Charlie looked at her expression and flashed back fifteen years. Ashley had worn this expression and had used the same arm-around-the-shoulder routine when she'd had to break the news that the family dog had disappeared.

Panic set in, tightening her chest. "Is Mark okay?"

"Mark's fine," Ashley said.

"Then what's the problem?"

All the women faced her now, each regarding her with pity. Something was definitely wrong, but instinct told her she didn't want to know what it was or even who these people were. Their logo was a donkey kicking some poor guy clear into next week, and DOA was spelled out in large white letters above the picture. Kind of gruesome all the way around, she thought.

"There might not be a problem," Ashley said. She kept her arm snugly around Charlie. "But you owe it to yourself to hear what they have to say."

The tall brunette with striking gray eyes stepped forward. She had an air of polish and authority about her. "Charlie, I'm Deb Creighton," she said. "I guess you could call me the ringleader." Then she turned to the other four and introduced each one.

Still totally confused, Charlie listened as Deb introduced Carrie, the redhead on the end with the wire-framed glasses. She looked like the intellectual of the group. Next to her was Jenna, who wore her long blond hair loose around her shoulders and looked as if she'd be happiest spending time on the Gulf, catching rays. Then came Phyllis, a slender woman with shiny black hair, and Hannah, an athletic-looking type whose taffy-colored hair was nearly as short as Charlie's.

Looking closer, Charlie saw that each one of the women had her name embroidered on her shirt, along with a date. Aside from wearing these team shirts, the women had one other thing in common—they were all very attractive. Extremely attractive. Charlie wondered if they'd been in the same beauty pageant which they'd won in the year stitched onto the purple material.

After making the introductions, Deb cleared her throat. "So here's the deal. On Monday I found out that Mark O'Grady proposed to you over the weekend."

Ashley's fingers tightened on her shoulder and Charlie's stomach pitched. "That's true," she said.

Deb looked her straight in the eye. "We're here to try and talk you out of it. You see, we—"

"Talk me out of it? Why on earth would—"

"Listen to their story," Ashley said. "Then you'll know."

"In the past seven years," Deb continued, "Mark has made and then canceled wedding plans with each of us. I'm the latest victim."

Charlie gasped. This couldn't be happening. She was having a horrible nightmare and any minute she'd wake up.

"In my case," Deb went on relentlessly, "he called it off ten minutes before the ceremony."

Charlie clutched her stomach. "Ten minutes?"

"I got two days' notice," said Jenna with a flip of her blond hair.

"I got one," said Phyllis.

Carrie adjusted her glasses and held up her hand, fingers outstretched. "Five hours."

"I was the luckiest," Hannah said. "I had four whole days advance notice."

Charlie wanted to run, but she felt weighed down, as if she might be dreaming this. She prayed that she was.

"I know this is a shock," Deb said, her gaze filled with compassion. "But, believe me, every single one of us would have given anything to know in advance, so that we could have avoided the heartbreak and humiliation."

Everyone nodded in agreement.

"But we've all been where you are." Phyllis tucked her dark hair behind her ears. "And we know that breaking off with him will be tough. Let's face it, he's fantastic in bed."

Charlie blushed. If this was a dream, that part was true enough.

"That's the hell of it," said Deb. "He's *wonderful* in bed. The best any of us has ever had. It's hard to totally despise the guy when he's...well, so talented in that area. Unfortunately, he has this bad habit of proposing after your first night together and then, when you're down to the wire, he cancels the wedding. Apparently he loves to get engaged, hates to get married."

Charlie's head began to hurt.

"He's a serial fiancé," said Jenna.

Charlie put her fingers to her pounding temples. "I can't...I can't believe this. I can't believe that what he said to me...was all a lie."

"Oh, it wasn't all a lie," said Deb. "He believes every word when he says it. But then he changes his mind. After I quit crying, I decided to track down his other fiancées, who all still lived in the Houston area, and we formed this support group."

"It's been wonderful for all of us," said Hannah. "We meet once a month, rotating among our apartments. We talk, drink wine, eat take-out, play Uno, trash Mark."

"Driving down to Austin to warn you is our first official project," said Carrie, earnestly peering at her through her glasses. "We're here to support you, to help you be strong, to make you see what has to be done. We can't let him claim another one of our own."

Charlie stared at them, feeling numb. "I can't believe it. I just can't believe it. He loves me!"

Deb nodded, her eyes full of sympathy. "I'm sure he does. For now. Until he decides that something about you just won't do. Then it's *adios, muchacha.*"

"No." Charlie shook her head. "He wouldn't do that.

We've been writing to each other for three months. We've discussed *everything*."

"Did you discuss his mother?" Deb asked quietly.

A chill went through her. "I know...I know he wants to tell her after we're married instead of inviting her." She realized how damning that information was, now.

"I was number three," Carrie said gently. "After he jilted me, his mother refused the invitation for the next two. She told him to let her know after the marriage license had been signed, and she'd welcome her new daughter-in-law. She was tired of getting emotionally involved with us and then having to cut us loose again."

Charlie wished it didn't all make sense. But it did. Sometime during their wonderful night together, she'd told herself that Mark was too good to be true. Apparently he was. She gazed dully at their T-shirts. She was afraid to ask, but she had to know. "What do those letters stand for?"

Deb's gaze was unflinching. "Damn O'Grady's Ass."

8

AFTER CHARLIE FINALLY convinced the DOAs to go back to Houston by promising them she'd stay in touch, she collapsed into the Queen Anne chair Ashley kept beside the three-way mirror. She'd never felt this tired, not even after her rim-to-rim hike through the Grand Canyon. But underneath her exhaustion boiled red-hot fury.

Ashley knelt in front of her and clasped both her hands. "Go ahead and cry, sweetie."

"I don't feel like crying." Her voice was tight and hard. "I feel like sending him over Niagara Falls in a barrel. And I will, once my muscles start working again."

"If that's what you want, I'll help you."

Charlie gazed at her sister and wondered what was strange about Ashley's reaction. Then she realized that Ashley didn't sound angry. Given the circumstances, she would have expected Ashley to be rounding up a posse and heading for Houston to avenge her little sister's honor.

What was it Ashley had said before the women dropped their bombshell? *There might not be a problem.* Yet when she'd said that, she'd known all about Mark's five broken engagements.

Ashley squeezed her hands. "I can tell you're still in

shock. Let's go down the street and order up a couple of *margaritas grande*. That should help."

"Okay. But how come you're so calm?" Charlie stared at her in bewilderment. "Why aren't you foaming at the mouth? Or saying *I told you so*? Could anything be much worse than this?"

Ashley took a deep breath. "Not on the surface of it, no. But those women had been here close to an hour before you showed up. In that time I had a chance to scope them out, and none of them are like you."

Charlie's laugh was bitter. "They're all gorgeous, if that's what you mean. I feel pretty damned insecure knowing Mark was engaged to that bunch."

"You're gorgeous, too," Ashley said. "But putting that aside for now, keep in mind that he didn't marry any of them. Maybe you're his type and none of them are. I don't think you should be too hasty, here."

Charlie's jaw dropped. Then she began making the points she'd expected Ashley to be ticking off. "Look, we don't know for an absolute certainty that I'm his type, and his record is five canceled weddings."

"I know, but—"

"Worse than that, he's been writing to me for three months, and in all that time he failed to mention this. Then he made love to me, *and* proposed, right on schedule. Obviously that's his M.O. I can reasonably expect him to cancel this wedding, too. Why wouldn't he?"

"Because Sam had a hand in the matchmaking this time."

"I know that. Mark told me the magazine ad was Sam's idea. So what? That only means Sam's an accomplice to the crime." She peered at Ashley with growing suspicion. "Did Sam tell you about all these engagements? Because if he did, and you didn't tell me, I'll—"

"No, he didn't tell me," Ashley said quickly. "But he did mention that Mark had been having a little trouble finding someone he could be ready to make a lifetime commitment to."

"A *little* trouble? That's like saying Alaska has a little trouble growing coconuts!" Charlie's energy returned. "Forget the margaritas. Let's drive up to Houston right now. I'm ready to do some serious damage to a certain stockbroker, and I have phone numbers for several women who will help me."

"We can if you want." Ashley stood and started pacing. "But before we head off, stop and think. Why do you think Mark put that ad in the magazine? He obviously can get dates without advertising."

In the past half hour, Charlie had become quite cynical. "We don't know that, either. I'll bet the word is out on him in Houston. He probably can't get a date there anymore, so he needed the magazine to find new victims."

"I don't think so. I think Sam helped him analyze the problem, and the magazine was the answer. From what Sam said, the two of them took it very seriously, combing through the letters until they came up with you, someone who seemed perfectly matched to him. I think it's possible that they concocted this whole project to make sure there were no more broken engagements."

"Then why didn't he tell me that?"

"I'm guessing he was afraid to," Ashley said. "What would you have done if he'd confessed everything in his letters? Would you have been as excited about getting to know him?"

Charlie had to admit that she likely would have been turned off by the information. Before she'd met him, knowing such a thing might have made her much more

The Harlequin Reader Service® — Here's how it works:

Accepting your 2 free books and gift places you under no obligation to buy anything. You may keep the books and gift and return the shipping statement marked "cancel." If you do not cancel, about a month later we'll send you 4 additional novels and bill you just $3.34 each in the U.S., or $3.80 each in Canada, plus 25¢ shipping & handling per book and applicable taxes if any.* That's the complete price and — compared to cover prices of $3.99 each in the U.S. and $4.50 each in Canada — it's quite a bargain! You may cancel at any time, but if you choose to continue, every month we'll send you 4 more books, which you may either purchase at the discount price or return to us and cancel your subscription.

*Terms and prices subject to change without notice. Sales tax applicable in N.Y. Canadian residents will be charged applicable provincial taxes and GST.

If offer card is missing write to: Harlequin Reader Service, 3010 Walden Ave., P.O. Box 1867, Buffalo NY 14240-1867

NO POSTAGE
NECESSARY
IF MAILED
IN THE
UNITED STATES

BUSINESS REPLY MAIL
FIRST-CLASS MAIL   PERMIT NO. 717   BUFFALO, NY

POSTAGE WILL BE PAID BY ADDRESSEE

HARLEQUIN READER SERVICE
3010 WALDEN AVE
PO BOX 1867
BUFFALO NY 14240-9952

Play The Lucky Hearts Game

and get...

FREE BOOKS & a FREE GIFT... YOURS to KEEP!

yes! I have scratched off the silver card. Please send me my **2 FREE BOOKS** and **FREE MYSTERY GIFT**. I understand that I am under no obligation to purchase any books as explained on the back of this card.

Scratch Here!
then look below to see
what your cards get you...

342 HDL DC32 **142 HDL DC3R**

NAME   (PLEASE PRINT CLEARLY)

ADDRESS

APT.#   CITY

STATE/PROV.   ZIP/POSTAL CODE

Twenty-one gets you
2 FREE BOOKS and a
FREE MYSTERY GIFT!

Twenty gets you
2 FREE BOOKS!

Nineteen gets you
1 FREE BOOK!

TRY AGAIN!

Visit us online at
www.eHarlequin.com

wary. They certainly wouldn't have spent the night together on the first date.

Thinking about that night made her even madder. She'd been a lamb to the slaughter, dazzled by the luxury of the room, the luxury of an excellent lover. The Presidential Suite, indeed. "He should have told me before he proposed."

Ashley nodded. "I agree. And I don't want to keep making excuses for him. Still, it would be a difficult subject to bring up." She sighed. "Maybe I shouldn't even be saying all these things. If you're ready to break it off with him, then do it. I wouldn't blame you. Nobody would."

"Some people would throw me a party." She gave Ashley a world-weary smile. "The DOAs are dying to have Mark be on the receiving end of a canceled wedding. Did you hear Deb ask if I'd consider going along with the wedding until five minutes before the ceremony?"

"Yes, and it's not your job to be the vehicle of their revenge. I can understand their feelings, but this is your life."

Charlie would love to accept all of Ashley's arguments, but she was so afraid she'd end up wearing a purple T-shirt. "You said none of them were like me. How were they different?" she asked finally.

"Well, Deb has a serious cell phone habit which drove me nuts, so I can imagine it would bother Mark. Jenna, the one with the long blond hair and the nice tan, is a shopaholic. She bought several hundred dollars' worth of stuff in no time and stashed it in the van. I think she would have bought more except her credit card was maxed out at that point."

A dim ray of hope began to penetrate Charlie's despair. "Mark and I discussed cell phones and excessive shopping in our letters."

Ashley gazed at her. "See? He's trying not to make another mistake."

"But what about Hannah, the one with the short hair? She looked athletic, like she could be an outdoor person, a hiker and camper."

"Well, she's not." Ashley leaned against the counter. "I wondered about her, too, so I asked. She prefers gyms. I also heard her scolding Jenna about buying so much, sort of like she was her mother or something. Some guys don't mind that kind of overprotective attitude, but Mark might."

"He does. He told me he hates being nagged."

Ashley nodded. "There you go. I think the guy is trying to work this out, Charlie."

"Maybe." Charlie sighed. "Of course I'd love to believe that, but I don't know, sis." She massaged her temples. "Tell me about the other two."

"Carrie, the one with the glasses, is very sweet, but she needs to find someone who's as excited about ancient languages as she is. It's all she talks about. As for Phyllis, the sleek, dark-haired one, she hates camping even more than the rest, but not a single one likes it."

Charlie turned all the information over in her mind. She couldn't deny that Mark had discussed these very things in his letters, although he'd never mentioned former girlfriends, and certainly not ex-fiancées. But then she hadn't named names when she'd brought up a few of her pet peeves. That hadn't seemed necessary.

"I don't mean to imply they're not all terrific women," Ashley said. "But Deb needs somebody who's into cell phone communication, and Jenna had better find either a millionaire or somebody who can put her on a budget. Some guys like to be mothered, and Hannah would be perfect for someone like that. Carrie ought to date only college professors in her field, and Phyllis should stick with urban types."

Charlie stood and walked over to the glass door of the shop to stare out at the traffic going by. She wondered if everyone else had this much trouble finding Mr. or Ms. Right. "I still wish he'd told me about all this before he proposed," she said.

"I do, too." Ashley came over and put her arm around her. "Maybe he's planning to confess everything this weekend when you go camping."

"Maybe he is, but that doesn't change the fact that he's canceled five weddings right before the ceremony. Maybe there's something about me that will turn him off and he'll cancel this one, too."

"You could postpone."

Charlie's gut tightened. "That doesn't feel like the solution. I'd only be dragging out the suspense."

"Then stop seeing him."

Her head told her to do that. Her heart rebelled. "I probably should, but I...damn it, I don't want to. Not if there's a chance this could be for real."

"Then I have a suggestion," Ashley said. "This weekend you could be a pain in the butt."

Charlie glanced at her. "Excuse me?"

Ashley turned, a conspiratorial light in her eyes. "Whether his intentions are good or bad, he deserves to catch some grief for not telling you the whole truth."

"He sure does," Charlie said with feeling.

"Then go camping with him, but don't be the perfect companion. You could pretend to be sick, refuse to have sex with him and put him through a miserable weekend of playing nursemaid."

Charlie's heart began to lift a little. Torturing Mark sounded much better than cutting off all contact. "I could forget the wine and burn the food. I could make sure there were rocks under his side of the tent."

"You could slather mosquito repellent on yourself and then forget where you put the bottle."

"I could accidentally dump water on his sleeping bag."

Ashley grinned. "You're getting the idea. And all the time you're waiting to see if he confesses, you can test the heck out of his commitment."

"In other words, I'll make his life a living hell for two days and see if he cracks."

"That's right."

Charlie began to smile, too. "I could get into that."

CAMPING WITH the woman of his dreams was going to be heaven, Mark thought as they neared the turnoff to the campground. At the perfect moment, maybe as they were lying naked in the tent after making love, he'd give her the engagement ring he'd bought this week.

He'd agonized over the stone and setting, but he thought he had it right. A ring box would have been too awkward to tuck in his jeans pocket, so he'd asked for a small velvet pouch, instead.

He could hardly wait for the moment he would slip the ring on her finger. He'd left work early so they could score a campsite before dark. Fortunately the weather was unseasonably cool and the wildflowers hadn't started blooming yet.

Although he would have loved to spend their first outing surrounded by bluebonnets and Indian paint brush, they'd have been surrounded by hundreds of other campers, as well.

Better to have some privacy. In fact, he was hoping for lots of privacy. As he pulled the Lexus into the sparsely populated campground, pleasure surged through him at the prospect of spending nearly two full days with Charlie.

She hadn't been very chatty on the drive out here, but he wasn't the kind of guy who liked constant conversation. Carrie's nonstop monologues used to make him desperate for silence.

Besides, he imagined Charlie might be a little tired after spending the week backpacking with two different groups. Before they'd left he'd offered her the option of checking into a luxury hotel instead. He'd been so eager to have a camper for a fiancée that he hadn't considered that this could be a busman's holiday for her.

But his Charlie was a real trouper. She'd insisted they go camping as planned, and had guided him to one of her favorite spots in the hill country. The rolling, tree-studded landscape fed his soul after spending five days in the city. He felt privileged to be here with her.

Sam hadn't been so lucky this weekend. He'd hoped to spend time with Ashley, but he'd been called out of town on business. They'd have to wait until the wedding to resume their relationship.

Charlie surveyed the sites as Mark drove slowly through the campground. "Let's take that one over there." She pointed to a vacant spot near a shallow creek.

"Looks perfect." He pulled into the adjacent parking area and wondered how quickly they could set up the tent. Six days without holding Charlie had made him very eager. He'd discovered that even when Charlie dressed in jeans and a flannel shirt, she made his mouth water. He shut off the engine and reached for the door handle.

"No, wait. Maybe that one over there would be better." She pointed to one farther down the road.

"Okay." He didn't much care. He just wanted to get the tent up. Starting the engine, he backed out and drove a few hundred yards down to the next site. He didn't think it was quite as picturesque, but he didn't plan to spend much time admiring the scenery.

Once again he killed the engine and opened the door to get out. God, but it smelled great—a combination of wood smoke, dried leaves and the evergreen scent of cypress down by the creek. And Charlie liked being here. He was so lucky to have found her.

"I was wrong," Charlie said. "The other site is better."

"Good. I think so, too." So she was being a little indecisive today. Everyone was entitled to that once in a while. In no time at all they'd have set up camp, and then...then he could start making love to this wonderful woman. After that, he'd slip the ring on her finger.

He backed out and drove to her original choice.

"You know, maybe this is too close to the creek," she said. "It might be colder and damper than the other one."

He chuckled. Yeah, he knew what this was all about. She wanted their first camping experience to be perfect, and neither one of these spots was perfect, because no site would be.

Turning off the engine, he gave her a tender smile. "Either of these sites will be like Shangri-La if you're here with me. Next to the creek, or not so close to the creek, it makes no difference. So you can stop worrying about it, okay?"

"Okay."

He'd expected her to smile back, but she didn't. "Charlie, is something wrong? Because if you don't like either of these sites, we can go looking some more. I just thought—"

"I was thinking the creek might make too much noise."

"Too much noise? Didn't you tell me you loved the sound of gurgling water?"

"As long as I don't have a headache."

"And you have a headache?"

"Uh-huh."

"Well, damn." He reached over and stroked her cheek. "Have you taken anything for it?"

"Not yet. It just came on a little while ago."

His hopes for a quick setup and immediate gratification began to dwindle. Not only that, he wasn't about to give her a ring when she wasn't feeling well. "Did you bring anything for a headache?" He knew he hadn't. Camping always took away his headaches, so he never had the need.

"I'm pretty sure I have something in my backpack."

"Then let's get it." He popped the trunk and was out of the car in no time. For some reason he hadn't figured a headache into his plans. But people got headaches, after all. And maybe in an hour or so hers would be gone. He'd waited six days. He could wait another hour.

Opening the ice chest stowed in the trunk, he took out a bottle of water and carried it, along with her backpack, up to the passenger side of the car. She hadn't opened the door yet, so he did it.

Then he crouched down next to her seat. "Tell me where to look, and I'll get the pills out for you."

She opened her eyes and turned her head toward him.

His breath caught. She was so beautiful, and her lips so full and sweet. They'd shared one brief kiss when he'd picked her up. It hadn't been near enough. "I've heard that having a good orgasm can cure a headache," he said softly.

A response stirred in her eyes. But then she sat up and took the backpack from him. "Thanks, but I think I'll go with ibuprofen this time." She zipped open a compartment in the backpack and sifted through the contents.

He tried not to feel rejected. He'd had headaches before, and they could really make you cranky. When she came up with a small container of capsules, he took the cap off the water and handed her the bottle. "Here you go."

"Thanks." She tossed a couple of pills in her mouth and swallowed some of the water.

He'd had such hopes for this weekend. Waking up this morning and looking forward to their trip, he'd felt like a kid on Christmas morning. But there would be other camping trips. He could live with a change of plans.

"Listen," he said. "If you're not feeling up to par, maybe we should go back."

"That's okay. I'm sure I'll be fine in a little while."

He laid his palm over her forehead. "At least you don't seem to have a fever." He allowed his hand to linger there, just for the excuse of touching her. "Tell you what. You sit here and relax, and I'll get the tent up and the sleeping bags inside. Then you can go in and lie down while I look for wood."

He liked that scenario. Maybe by the time he came

back with firewood, she'd have recovered. And the tent would be ready and waiting....

"No, I want to help you with the tent. Since it's mine, I know how it goes up." She unsnapped her seat belt.

So did he. His small dome tent was the same kind as hers, but he decided not to argue with her. Headaches could really make a person irrational if they were bad enough.

They'd set up the tent together, and then he'd see that she was tucked inside shortly thereafter. He had a feeling if he could once get her into the tent and on top of a camping mattress and a fluffy sleeping bag, everything would start to work out.

In a few minutes they'd unrolled the tent on the ground in what looked like a reasonable spot to him. Once again he took a deep breath of the sweet-smelling air. Waking up in this place, with Charlie tucked in beside him, would be beyond his wildest dreams.

"I think we should put it over there," she said.

Boy, she was being *really* indecisive today. He decided to blame it on the headache, which was probably a result of tension. After all, they were getting married next week. Maybe she was freaking out about that. But some good lovemaking would loosen her up in no time.

He'd promised himself he'd tell her about his five broken engagements this weekend, but he couldn't tell her until she felt better. When he finally spread his messy background out for her to see, he wanted her to be in a wonderful mood and wearing his ring, not nursing a headache.

Until then he'd do what he could to make her happy. So he helped her drag the tent to a new spot. A rockier spot, from his quick inspection. "Charlie, I think the other place was flatter and softer."

She put her hands on her hips and glanced from the previous tent site to this one.

He took that moment to admire the way her posture emphasized her slim hips and full breasts. He wished she'd unfasten a button or two of her flannel shirt, but he could wait for her to turn into his little temptress again.

She would, once her headache was gone. The fading sunlight stroked her cap of blond curls, making her look as if she wore a halo. She was his angel. He was convinced of that.

"Nope," she said. "This is the best place."

He didn't agree, and it could become a problem if the rocks interfered with their fun and games later on. But if they did, it wouldn't be that hard to pull up stakes and move the tent. He'd done it a few times himself when he'd misjudged the location.

As he'd figured, the tent went up exactly like his, with two arched poles that crossed in the middle. But he let Charlie direct the action because she seemed to want to do that. Soon they had a nylon igloo-shaped structure that looked so inviting he wondered how he'd keep from trying to seduce her.

"Time for the mattresses and sleeping bags." She sounded totally matter-of-fact about it, as if she had no interest in what they might do once they covered the floor of the small tent with a soft layer of bedding.

"How's your head feel?" he asked as they walked back to the car for the rest of the gear.

"I'm afraid it's worse."

"Oh." Well, that could explain why she wasn't acting interested in sex. But headaches went away. He could wait this one out. He could even wait until morning, if absolutely necessary.

Or maybe not. He paused as Charlie leaned over to pull a sleeping bag out of the back seat. The sight of those snug jeans and the memory of what was inside them left him shaking.

Now he was even more glad they'd chosen the site near the stream, because if her headache didn't disappear very soon, he might have to go sit in it and cool his crotch.

9

AS AN OUTDOOR ADVENTURE GUIDE Charlie had endured her share of hardships. She'd capsized while white-water rafting on the Arkansas River, banged her head against a rock and suffered a mild concussion. She'd fallen on a mountain-climbing expedition in the Grand Tetons, broken her ankle, and had hobbled to civilization using a tree branch as a crutch. She'd been bitten by a rattlesnake in the bottom of the Grand Canyon while out hiking alone, which meant she'd had to treat her own bite, an extremely unpleasant experience.

Yet she'd never suffered as much with any of those disasters as she was suffering now. Having Mark this close and not allowing herself to make love to him took more guts and discipline than anything she'd ever attempted in her life.

She'd counted on being angrier on this trip. But no matter how many times she reminded herself that he'd proposed without revealing his disreputable past, she still couldn't maintain enough righteous indignation to neutralize the effect of those deep brown eyes.

When he'd shown up at her door wearing a long-sleeved denim shirt, jeans and hiking boots, she'd nearly swooned with pleasure. He'd looked yummy all dressed up when they'd met at the restaurant, but she'd already decided she preferred this rugged image.

Of course he'd tried to engage her in a long, passionate kiss. Breaking away from that dizzying embrace had almost killed her, but she'd done it, telling him that they had to get moving if they expected to set up before dark.

They'd planned an easy car-camping experience for this first time, but even so they'd had to drive a ways before reaching the campground. She'd spent most of that drive staring out the window, because whenever she looked at Mark she wanted to grab him and kiss him until they were both breathless.

Now here they were, in a fairly deserted park, and the sexual tension was wearing her down quickly. For one thing, camping had always appealed to her. Maybe it was a holdover from her childhood when she'd made tents in the backyard, but the idea of setting up a temporary shelter in the woods seemed so incredibly cozy.

Lying cocooned inside a nylon dome listening to the wind in the trees, the babble of the water in the creek and the hoot of an owl had always given her tremendous pleasure. Add to that having the man she adored ready to crawl into the tent with her, and the pleasure potential increased almost beyond bearing.

She'd nearly given up the fight and thrown herself in his arms about ten times. Now she found herself walking toward that little tent clutching a sleeping bag and a self-inflating camping mattress so she could create a bed.

They couldn't work together on this. Putting up the tent had been torture enough, with accidental brushing of bodies and touching of hands. Laying down mattresses and sleeping bags would involve way too much close contact, not to mention the urges she'd have once the floor of the tent became a cushy mattress. When he'd suggested that a good orgasm might get rid of her supposed headache, she'd nearly abandoned the whole program.

"It's getting dark and you'll have trouble finding firewood if you don't go now," she said over her shoulder. "You should probably leave the sleeping bag and mattress setup to me."

"I can help. It won't take long."

She would just bet he'd help—help dissolve all her resistance until she was naked and willing. But no matter how much that appealed to her, she had a job to do this weekend. She was testing him, and falling into his arms wouldn't provide much of a test.

"I'm cold, Mark," she said. What a big fat lie that was. "I'd really like you to get a fire going as soon as possible."

"Oh." He set down his sleeping bag and mattress on the campsite's concrete picnic table. "All right. But why not sit and relax while I get firewood? I can finish the setup when I get back."

"I'd like to get it done." She crouched down and put her rolled sleeping bag and mattress inside the tent.

He came to stand beside her and cupped the back of her head gently. "Don't forget to zip them together," he said softly.

How she longed to lean into his light caress and respond with the loving words he wanted to hear. In their letters they'd compared notes on sleeping bags to make sure theirs were compatible and actually would zip together.

But she was planning to sabotage all that. "I forgot to tell you," she said, "my other sleeping bag got trashed. I don't think this one's zipper is the same size as yours. We'll each have to be in our own bag."

He was silent for a moment. Then he crouched down

next to her. "Charlie, what's the problem?" he asked gently.

Her pulse rate shot up. When he used that tone of voice with her, she had trouble thinking straight. All she wanted was to be in his arms. "Nothing's the problem." She pulled off the cinch around her rolled mattress and unfurled it on the tent floor.

"I think there is. You're acting...different. If something's wrong, then we need to talk about it. "

"Nothing to talk about." She didn't dare turn her head to look at him, so she kept working, unfastening the straps on her sleeping bag and unrolling it on top of her mattress.

"I can understand that you might have the jitters about next weekend. It's a big step. But I think we're ready for it."

She was ready for something now. His tenderness reminded her of his soft murmurs when he was deep inside her. Where was her anger when she needed it?

She stood and left him crouched there while she walked over to get his mattress from the picnic table. "I have a headache, and my sleeping bag got wrecked. No big deal."

He sighed and rose to his feet. "Okay. I'll go get firewood."

No matter how she lectured herself, the confusion and sadness in his voice tore at her heart. For weeks they'd looked forward to spending time together in this setting, and she was deliberately spoiling it.

She took a deep breath. Okay. He'd already jilted five women. She didn't want to be number six. Unrolling his mattress, she positioned it over the bed of rocks under his side of the tent floor. The mattress wasn't nearly thick enough to cushion him from those rocks.

She unrolled his sleeping bag on top of the mattress before going in search of her water bottle. Then she climbed into the tent, nudged off her shoes, and zipped the flap closed as a subtle Do Not Disturb sign. After positioning the water bottle so it would gradually leak into his sleeping bag, she crawled fully clothed into her own, all the while feeling extremely underhanded. But he'd been underhanded, too. She had to remember that.

Not long after she'd settled into the sleeping bag, she heard the steady thwack, thwack of an ax biting into dead branches. Pretending to have a sick headache meant she couldn't watch Mark as he played Paul Bunyan. Damn. The sight of a gorgeous man chopping firewood got her juices flowing. Some women might fall for a bouquet of roses, but Charlie was a sucker for a stack of expertly chopped wood.

She could handle the chore herself, of course, usually better than the guys that she'd taken camping. Many times after watching them bungle through the job, she'd taken over. And she'd tried not to judge their manliness on that specific skill. She really had tried. Yet she could tell from the rhythm of Mark's strokes that he knew what he was doing in this area, too. Her delight had a definite sexual tinge to it.

Soon she identified the familiar crackle of a fire and smelled wood smoke. She adored the smell of wood smoke. Sitting beside a campfire with someone you liked ranked high on her list. Sitting beside it with someone you desperately wanted to make love to would be spectacular.

She hoped that someday they'd have a wonderful camping trip. But first she needed to find out what Mark O'Grady was made of. Surely this weekend he'd tell her about his ex-fiancées.

The muted clatter of pans indicated that he'd decided to leave her alone for a while and start dinner. His attempts to be quiet while he worked touched her. He really seemed to care. She'd grabbed a quick snack before he'd arrived to pick her up so that she could pretend not to be hungry. But as a delicious aroma drifted into the tent, she wondered if her mouth would water and give her away.

Moments later the zipper on the front flap slid open. "Charlie?" he called softly. "Would you like a cup of cocoa?"

She stifled a moan of disappointment, knowing she couldn't respond to the incredibly sweet gesture. He'd obviously remembered her saying how much she loved the stuff, and he was hoping a cup would make her feel better.

"Charlie?" he murmured again.

"Thanks for the thought, but I guess not," she said.

"How's your head?"

"Not great."

Silence followed her answer. Then he spoke with more determination. "Look, let's pack up and go back. This could be the start of something worse. I don't want to take chances with your health just because we planned this camping trip."

"I'll be fine," she said. "All I need is some sleep. I'll probably be much better in the morning. Go ahead and fix yourself some dinner."

"I don't think we should stay." There was no impatience in his voice, only concern.

"I do. Please, Mark, let's just wait it out tonight. If I'm worse in the morning, we can go back."

"Okay. We'll wait and see." He paused. "I love you," he said.

The words zinged through her, shaking her determination. She swallowed the sudden lump in her throat. "I love you, too," she said.

"That's all that matters," he murmured. "Sleep well." He put down the mug of cocoa and zipped the flap closed again.

As she lay there listening to his dinner preparations, she wondered if he'd consider spending the night in the car. For all he knew she had something contagious, and sleeping with her in the tent might be hazardous to his own health. She'd known men who were finicky about that, and it wasn't something she and Mark had ever talked about in their letters, maybe because they were both pretty healthy.

How to deal with sickness might be the only thing they hadn't covered in those letters. They'd hashed out the issue of children and thought two would be a good number. As for child care, they believed in keeping their respective jobs and cutting back equally when babies arrived. Other hot topics had also been dissected—spiritual beliefs, financial attitudes, politics.

She'd thought they'd probed into everything two people needed to know before they made a commitment. She'd thought her knowledge of this man eclipsed her understanding of anyone else she'd ever dated. Yet Mark hadn't told her that he'd come within a hair's breadth of being married—five times. There was no getting around it. That omission was huge.

And so she forced herself to be strong as she lay in the tent listening to Mark washing up the dishes. Later on, when she pictured him sitting by himself while he stared into the fire and longed for her, she clenched her jaw and vowed not to leave the tent and join him.

When at last the zipper on the tent flap slid open

again, she pretended to be asleep. She kept her eyes closed and her breathing shallow as he rustled around getting ready for bed. Now she'd learned something else about him. He wasn't afraid of whatever germs she was carrying. Maybe that wasn't wise, but she appreciated his nobility in staying with her even when she could be contagious.

Of course he might be staying with her because he hoped she'd miraculously wake up cured and they could engage in their favorite activity. But that wasn't going to happen. Ashley's final instructions were *don't have sex.* Considering how sex impaired Mark's judgment, it was excellent advice. Difficult advice, but excellent.

She judged from all the rustling around that he was taking off most of his clothes. *Or all of his clothes.* Her breath hitched at that thought.

"Charlie?" he whispered. "Are you awake?"

She didn't answer. But her body certainly did. His scent filled the tent, arousing her with potent memories of the last time they'd shared a bed. Her skin tingled, her nipples tightened and a sweet ache settled between her thighs.

No one had ever given her the kind of loving Mark had. She could understand why his other fiancées had held on to the relationship, even when incompatibility reared its ugly head. Any woman lucky enough to be in bed with Mark would be tempted to rationalize away any problems they might have out of bed.

When he slipped into his sleeping bag and drew in a quick breath, she knew he'd made contact with the soggy lining. He fumbled around until he encountered the water bottle. A tiny bit of water sloshed as he set it somewhere else. Most of the bottle had drained onto the flannel interior of his sleeping bag.

Maybe now he'd sleep in the car. His sleeping bag was wet and no doubt by now he could feel the rocks under his side of the tent. She'd chosen this location on purpose because she'd been able to direct the tent setup so that her side was smooth and his rocky.

But he stayed. Soggy sleeping bag, rocks and potential germs notwithstanding, he stayed. When he rested his hand lightly on her shoulder, she somehow managed to control the quiver of awareness. His touch was heaven and hell, all rolled into one.

She wondered if he'd go further with the gentle caress. If only he would. She'd rebuff him, of course, but she was supposed to be asleep, so her rebuff could take awhile.

He didn't go further. Apparently all he wanted was that connection, because he lay there perfectly still, his breathing steady, as if all he needed was to be by her side. She fought the urge to wiggle out of her sleeping bag and snuggle against him, or better yet, invite him into hers where it was dry.

She did neither. Instead, she lay listening to the forest and the creek. In her agitated state, the whisper of the trees and the murmur of the water sounded like lovers in the dark. Eventually she fell into a troubled sleep.

MARK AWOKE wrapped around Charlie, who was still covered from nose to toes in her sleeping bag. During the night he'd given up on the clammy interior of his and had decided to sleep on top of it. Then he'd instinctively snuggled close to Charlie for warmth.

It was like trying to hug a full laundry bag. And yet he knew a loving, sensuous woman lurked inside all that goose down, flannel and canvas. The top of her head was inches from his chin, and her short blond curls were tumbled as if she'd been in a wind tunnel.

Of course he had another erection this morning. Or maybe it was the same one he'd had when he'd finally drifted off to sleep. One erection just blended in with another so far this trip. He'd left his briefs and T-shirt on because he'd felt silly going to bed naked when his lover was fully clothed and swaddled in her sleeping bag.

His jeans, with the ring still in the pocket, lay folded at his feet along with his shirt. He hadn't planned for his clothes to be in a neat pile. He'd thought they'd be strewn everywhere, wrenched off in a frenzy of passion. The weekend was turning out very differently from what he'd expected.

But it was a new day. Pale light filtered through the tent seams and the birds had started tuning up outside. Charlie had said she expected her headache to be gone in the morning. It was morning. The sun was out, which meant he could put his sleeping bag outside and dry the place where Charlie's water bottle had leaked.

Sometime today they'd also move this tent to another spot. He felt as if he'd been sleeping on a torture board all night. But if Charlie woke up and wanted to make love, then he'd worry about moving the tent later. If opportunity knocked, he planned to be standing right by the door ready to fling it open.

She stirred. When she began to move, he relaxed his grip so that she could turn toward him. She was so buried in the sleeping bag that when she rolled over to face him, only her eyes peeked out. She looked like a blue-eyed bandit.

"Good morning." He couldn't help grinning at the

picture she made. "You look like Oscar the Grouch peering out of his garbage can."

Her eyes twinkled with laughter.

Oh, thank God. She's over her headache. "Actually, you look a whole lot better than that." He reached for the flap of the sleeping bag. As he drew it down below her chin, he brought her full, tempting lips out of hiding. His body began to hum eagerly in anticipation.

Without lipstick her mouth was the tender rose hue of the horizon at dawn. He decided that dawn was the perfect time to make love and give her the ring. "I never had the urge to kiss Oscar," he said.

The sparkle left her eyes. "You'd better not kiss me, either," she said. "My tummy doesn't feel so good. I might have the flu."

He gazed at her with longing while he fought his growing frustration. But it wasn't her fault if she was sick, and what she needed was understanding from him, not impatience. He tried to ignore the throbbing demands of his penis. "Does your head still hurt?" he asked.

"Not so much."

"Let's see if you have a fever." He laid his hand over her forehead and it was cool to the touch. Not wanting to lose even this little bit of physical contact, he moved from testing her forehead to combing his fingers through her hair. "No fever," he said.

"That's good."

He gave her scalp a gentle massage while he was at it. "Know what I think? I think it's an attack of matrimonial nerves."

"Well, I don't. I'm looking forward to this wedding."

"So am I. But I don't have much to do to get ready.

You do. I can understand why you'd be stressing about it."

"Not really," she said. "Ashley's been a huge help with our dresses and the flowers. And once I'd reserved the church and the restaurant for the reception, there wasn't a lot more to do. If we were having a big wedding, that would be something else, but we're not. Once you and I apply for the license on Monday morning, I think we're all set."

He loved hearing the wedding details. He also loved watching the movement of her mouth. He wouldn't mind *feeling* the movement of her mouth, either, but for some reason she was keeping him at arm's length. It had to be the stress.

"Maybe we're all set for the wedding, but you might be thinking about the upheaval when we get back from our honeymoon," he said. "You have to move to Houston. We've talked about looking for a house. All that could give anybody a headache and a bad tummy."

"Do you have stress?"

"About the wedding? No. I've never felt so convinced of something in my life as I am that we should get married." He was pretty stressed right now, lying with her in the tent without being able to strip her naked and lose himself in her warmth. But that was temporary stress. Her attack of nerves would go away eventually.

He did have a problem, however. If Charlie was nervous about the wedding, he couldn't imagine how to tell her about his five previous engagements this weekend. She'd back out for sure after hearing that.

The best thing to do was tell her after they were married, after he'd proven that this time was different. They only had a week to go. A week from today they'd pledge their eternal love and then head off for Jamaica. He'd tell her during the honeymoon, after she felt truly and completely married to him. Yes, that was the answer.

In the meantime, he'd just thought of a brilliant idea. "Let me give you a massage," he said. "A massage will boost your immune system, in case you have the flu. But if it's a case of wedding jitters, it'll help relax you."

If his previous experience with giving women massages was anything to go by, soon they'd both be extremely relaxed—not to mention sexually satisfied. Then he'd give her the ring, and all would be well.

"I'd rather not," she said. "In fact, I'm getting up." In no time she'd scrambled out of her sleeping bag, unzipped the tent flap and crawled out into the morning light.

Flopping back on his uncomfortable bed, he swore softly. He couldn't figure out how Charlie had gone from being one of the most cooperative women in the world to being one of the most frustratingly perverse.

She didn't seem really sick, so he must be right that her headache and stomach problems were related to wedding jitters. He might be responsible for her panic because he'd asked her to get married so quickly, but he had several stress-busters up his sleeve. She wasn't letting him use any of them, and that was raising his own stress level considerably.

He might as well get dressed now, though. She'd left the tent as if her tail was on fire, so he didn't think there was much chance she'd be crawling back in and asking him to give her that massage. Damn shame, too. He'd found that a good full-body massage was a natural segue into great sex.

Once he'd pulled on his clothes he crawled out of the

tent and discovered Charlie was building a fire. "I'll do that," he said.

"I know, but I'd like to." She added more kindling and struck a match. "I've felt so useless this trip. I'm going to cook you breakfast."

"That doesn't make sense if you have an upset stomach."

"Cooking will take my mind off it." The fire crackled to life. "And I'm tired of lying in that tent."

He wasn't surprised to hear that. He'd never intended their time in that tent to be so boring. But one thing was for sure. The woman knew her way around a campfire. Despite his frustration at their lack of sexual interaction, he was gratified to finally be with a woman who had outdoor skills. He hadn't realized until now how important that was to him.

Maybe the activity of cooking breakfast would help her work off her case of nerves. He sure hoped so, because every time she leaned over that fire, she touched off a blaze that threatened to drive him crazy.

10

CHARLIE WASN'T A GREAT COOK, but she enjoyed the challenge of turning out a meal using a campfire. She'd mastered bacon and eggs long ago because she happened to love eating them outdoors on a fresh, nippy morning like today. Add to that a cup of strong coffee, and she was in camper heaven.

But her purpose this weekend was to treat Mark to camper hell. Stage one involved screwing up the coffee by making it strong enough to eat through metal. She'd even pretend to enjoy it, and if he was a typical male, he wouldn't be able to admit that the coffee was too strong for him. She'd be totally wired for the rest of the day, but it was a small price to pay.

Carrying out her strategy took some concentration, which was good because Mark looked even more appealing this morning than he had the night before. She'd never seen him with such a manly growth of beard.

Apparently he'd shaved before their restaurant date this past weekend, so even though they'd spent the entire night together, his beard hadn't had time to grow out much by the next morning. But this morning was a different story. Every time she glanced in his direction he looked even more rugged and sexy than he had a moment ago. Her pulse was in permanent overdrive and her juices were flowing.

And then, oh, Lordy, he decided to chop more wood for the fire. Rolling back his sleeves, he took a large dead branch he'd hauled in the night before, propped it on a nearby stump, braced it with one foot, and began to reduce it to kindling-sized pieces.

As he worked rhythmically and efficiently, the muscles in his forearms bunched and his jeans pulled taut over his butt. Charlie stared at him, forgetting what she was doing until a hot cinder popped out of the fire and landed on her shirt.

She brushed it off and realized she'd lost count of the number of scoops she'd put in the coffee basket. She added some more for good measure and put the pot on the cooking grate.

Damn, but she wanted to make love to that guy. Watching him move around the campsite, she could hardly believe that they were engaged. A hunk who made her quiver with anticipation had said that he wanted to spend the rest of his life with her. But she had to remind herself that it might not come true.

She must not forget what she'd learned this week. Saying and doing might be two different things. Maybe he'd get cold feet the way he had five times before. Maybe something about her would turn him off and he'd call the whole thing off. It wasn't as if he wasn't capable of that.

So no matter how gorgeous he looked this morning, she had to put him through his paces. For starters, she could suggest he go find his razor. If he shaved off his beard so he didn't resemble a dashing pirate, then she might be able to resist grabbing him and pulling him into the tent with her.

The motor oil coffee was perking and she'd started her program of burning the bacon when he came over with an armload of wood. She turned to him with a smile. "I have this under control, if you want to go shave."

"Uh, sure." He set the wood down next to the fire pit. "Sure, I could do that," he said more eagerly. His eyes lit with excitement. "I'd be happy to shave."

She felt a little sorry for him. He probably thought he was shaving because she intended to make love to him after breakfast. But he might not feel so amorous after eating the breakfast she'd be serving.

As the scent of burning bacon filled the clearing, she wondered if he'd comment on it. When he didn't, she peeked over toward the picnic table where he'd set up his shaving gear. Uh-oh. Asking him to shave had clearly been a mistake. Now her love god was shirtless.

She gulped as memories of last weekend came flooding back. Her mouth remembered the taste and texture of his skin, the tickle of his chest hair, the shape of his nipples. The smell of charred bacon was strong, but not strong enough to block out the sweet aroma of his shaving cream, an aroma that brought back the moist pleasure of their first kiss. And their second kiss. And all the kisses thereafter.

The bacon had shriveled until it resembled rusty barbed wire by the time she wrenched her attention away from the sight of Mark stroking his razor over his deliciously square jaw. All the while he never gave any indication that he'd noticed the smell of burning meat. His nostrils had twitched a couple of times, but he'd continued to shave as if the bacon was no concern of his.

She'd begun to wonder who was torturing whom by the time she removed the stiff pieces of bacon and cracked the eggs into the pan. She broke the yokes and saturated the whole mess with salt. When the eggs were crisp as a scouring pad on the bottom, she flipped them over and fried the hell out of the other side. Mark would need to fetch his ax to make any headway with this grub.

Personally she was so hungry she might eat it if he didn't. Secretly, of course. When she'd been chortling over her plans with Ashley she'd failed to recognize that she'd have to suffer right along with Mark.

She used a spatula to dish the unappetizing concoction onto a tin plate, which she set down on the picnic table. "It might be a little overdone," she said.

"No problem." Mark finished buttoning his shirt and sat down.

"I'll get some coffee." She returned to the fire and used a potholder to pick up the blue spatter-ware pot. As she poured two matching mugs full to the brim, the sludge that came out of the pot looked exactly like the stuff the garage had drained from her crankcase a month ago.

She put the mug next to Mark's plate and took a seat across the table from him, both to keep her distance and to observe his reaction.

"Thanks for fixing all this," he said as he picked up his coffee mug. "You're sure you don't want any?"

"I'll stick with coffee for now." She held her breath.

He took a swallow from his mug. His eyes widened, but he somehow managed to turn a grimace into a smile. "Wow, that's robust."

"I like it strong."

"Yeah, me too." He took another gulp of the coffee.

If she hadn't been watching closely, she'd have missed his shudder when he swallowed it. She decided to see how bad it was and raised the mug to her lips. Although she'd braced herself for the taste, her mouth wasn't ready. She nearly gagged.

He was out of his seat and patting her back in no time. "Easy. It's pretty strong stuff."

"I think...I put in too much coffee," she rasped.

"That can happen." He crouched next to her as he continued to rub her back. "Are you okay?"

She nodded. "Uh-huh. Thanks." She had to make him stop rubbing her back before she begged him to rub her all over. He had the most magical touch of any man she'd ever known. "Now go ahead and eat your breakfast before it gets cold." *Or petrifies.*

"All right." He seemed reluctant as he went back to his seat, either because he'd hoped the back-rub might turn into something else, or because he wasn't looking forward to this meal.

She'd guess both.

But to his credit, he sat down, picked up a shrunken strip of bacon and bit off the end. His attempts to chew the bacon sounded like a rock tumbler in motion. Then he swallowed and smiled at her again. "Crisp."

She stared at him. Apparently he was going to eat the whole meal and not complain. "It's not just crisp. It's burned beyond recognition," she said.

"Guess so."

"You don't have to eat it."

"Sure I do. You made it for me." He bit off another section with a sharp crunch.

She watched in amazement as he polished off one strip of bacon and started in on his first egg. He had to use a steak knife to cut it. But cut it he did, and popped a bite into his mouth.

After some pretty fierce chewing, he swallowed the mouthful of egg. "Nice and firm," he said. "I hate it when they're too gooey." He picked up his knife and began sawing off another section.

"Wait." Consumed with guilt, she reached over and grabbed his wrist before he put any more of that breakfast atrocity in his mouth. "I can't stand this. Don't eat another bite."

He gazed at her, his brown eyes warm. "What if I want to?"

"Well, I *don't* want you to." She took a deep breath. "I made it terrible on purpose."

He shrugged. "I know."

Her jaw dropped. "You *know*?"

"Sure." He grinned at her. "Nobody with your camping experience could be that bad at cooking over an open fire. You laid it on too heavily to be convincing."

"I could *so* have been that bad!"

"Nope. If you'd barely burned the bacon, I would have believed it was an accident. If the eggs were a little brown around the edges, I would have figured you misjudged the heat. But the coffee was a tipoff. I know you like coffee. You go camping all the time, sometimes alone. There's no way you wouldn't have learned how to make a good pot of campfire coffee at the very least."

Her face grew hot. "Why didn't you say something?"

He continued to smile at her. "I figured if I ate it without complaining, you might give in and tell me you did it on purpose, which you just did."

Her face flaming with embarrassment, she stood and walked over to the fire pit. "I'll start over." She grabbed a potholder and picked up the frying pan. "I think we still have enough coals to—" She caught her breath as he circled her waist with one arm and took the frying pan with his free hand.

He set it back down on the edge of the fire pit and

wrapped his arm around her ribs, just under her breasts. His hold was gentle, but firm. There wasn't a trace of anger in his voice. "First I want to know why you did it."

Enclosed by his arms, with his breath warm on her neck, she felt her resistance ebbing way. A girl could only be so strong.

He leaned down and nuzzled the side of her neck. "And while you're at it, you can tell me why you've been deliberately avoiding having sex with me."

Oh, his lips felt so good against her skin. She closed her eyes and struggled to remember her game plan. "I haven't been—"

"Yes, you have." His tongue tickled the spot behind her earlobe. "At first I thought you were feeling under the weather because of wedding jitters. But after this breakfast stunt, I think you've been making up the sick part, too. How come, Charlie?"

She didn't know what to say, couldn't decide what to think, especially when he was playing havoc with her senses. The facts. What were the facts? He'd had dinner alone without complaint, slept on a bed of rocks in a soggy sleeping bag without protest, and had planned to eat her lousy breakfast.

After all that, she couldn't doubt his love and commitment. Not many men would have put up with her shenanigans, especially after they'd figured out her behavior was intentional. But he had, and now he didn't even sound upset—only concerned. And he was so warm. And she needed him so much.

She decided on a partial truth. "Maybe I don't quite believe that this is real. Maybe I needed to test you."

"I thought it might be something like that." He urged

her closer, letting her feel his erection as he nibbled her earlobe. "Did I pass?"

Sort of, she thought. Mmm. His hand felt so nice sliding between her thighs, rubbing her gently through the denim.

Still, he really should have told her about his broken engagements. But as he cupped her breast, she longed to rip her clothes off so he could do it right.

Maybe she should tell him she knew. Except now...now he'd unbuttoned her shirt and slipped his hand inside.

She shouldn't let him do this until he'd explained himself, because...because...oh, that felt so good....

"I still hear doubts whizzing around in your head," he murmured against her ear. "But I think the rest of you wants to give in and let me love you."

FOR YEARS HE'D KNOWN he had a gift for seduction. He'd never needed that gift more. He only knew one surefire way to erase Charlie's doubts about his commitment. When he was buried inside her, he was as committed as he'd ever been in his life, and he believed she knew it on some basic level. Then, when she'd been well and properly loved, he'd seal the bargain by giving her the ring in his pocket.

He'd enjoyed every minute of his sexual encounters with his ex-fiancées, but enjoyment was far too flimsy a word to describe what he felt when he sank into Charlie's warm, moist body. He hadn't realized that such a feeling existed, and he was still at a loss to describe it.

There was unity—and yet he was aware of her special individuality that meshed so well with his. There was surrender—and yet he gave up nothing and gained everything when he made love to her. There was peace—and yet energy surged through him at the moment of connection.

He needed all of those things now, and so did she. "Come to bed with me," he murmured.

And she did, tumbling with him through the tent flap, kissing him frantically, her mouth hot and needy as she wrestled him out of his clothes with as much urgency as he was using on hers. They started with the most essential things, tugging at the snaps and zippers of their jeans.

They shoved off their shoes along with the jeans and with breathless half words agreed to forget about taking off their shirts.

"I just want you inside me," she said.

"And I want to be there. God, do I want to."

"Condoms," she said, panting as she wiggled out of her panties. "Where did you put the condoms?"

He shucked off his briefs to reveal his rigid penis. His chest heaved as he tried to remember what he'd done with the blasted things. He'd remembered to keep tabs on the ring, but not the condoms. A guy could only keep track of so much, and the ring was a priority. "They might be in my backpack."

She groaned.

So much for a smooth seduction. If he put his clothes back on to go get a condom, he might give her a chance to cool down. She might decide to start playing games again to test him. But he had to have the condom.

Or did he?

He pushed her gently down onto the soft flannel of her open sleeping bag. "Let's forget the condom."

Her gaze locked with his for several seconds. Then she swallowed. "Forget it?"

"We're getting married in a week." Holding her

gaze, he moved over her. "You said you can hardly wait to have kids. Neither can I. We'll have great kids." His heart beat faster as he realized that this might be the perfect way to convince her that for both of them, there was no turning back.

She searched his expression, her blue eyes serious. "Are you sure you know what you're doing?"

"Yeah." He gave her a slow smile. "I'm about to knock you up."

She put a hand on his chest, holding him back. "I come from a long line of fertile women." She drew in a ragged breath. "You'd better be absolutely sure."

"That I want kids? You know I do. Two girls, or two boys, or one of each—I don't care. Let's start making them."

"I mean, you'd better be sure that you want to marry me."

He looked into her eyes and saw the doubts swirling there. "I'm sure," he said. "Are you sure?"

She nodded.

He sighed with relief. Her doubts were all about him, and he would make them go away. He would banish them forever.

"I want to marry you," he said softly. He leaned down and kissed her slowly and gently, telling her with his kiss how he felt. Then he lifted his head and gazed down at her so that he could use the words. "I love you."

The doubts began to fade from her eyes.

But he wanted them gone without a trace. "I've never made love to a woman without using birth control," he murmured, "because no matter how much I cared about her, I wasn't sure, not deep down in my gut, that she was my mate."

Slowly a light began to grow in her eyes. "And now you are?"

"Yes." He eased forward, closing his eyes with pleasure as the tip of his penis slid between the dew-drenched petals of her vagina. "Oh, yes."

She drew in a quick breath and clutched his hips.

He paused, opening his eyes. Then he held her gaze as he kept his penetration shallow, sliding slowly back and forth at the entrance to salvation. He wooed her as he never had any other woman.

Instead of empty, poetic phrases, he gave her the promises that mattered. Even if she didn't know that, he certainly did. "We're going to make it, Charlie," he said. "We're going to see each other through teething babies, grape juice on the rug, puppies in the flower bed, dings in the new car."

Tears glistened in her eyes. "We are?"

"We are. I thought so when we were writing to each other, but I knew it the minute I saw you. Believe in me, Charlie. Believe in me, my love."

Her voice was thick with emotion. "Oh, Mark. I do. I really do."

"That's all we'll ever need." In one smooth motion he thrust deep, and there it was, the feeling that went beyond words, the feeling he required more than life itself.

With a cry she lifted to meet him. "I love you," she whispered hoarsely.

"Just keep loving me." His throat constricted, and he blinked back his own tears. He'd convinced her. Dear God, he'd done it. "Just keep it up," he said in a husky voice, "because we're so good together."

"I know."

"So good." Still looking into her eyes, he settled into

a rhythm that was all their own. They'd found that rhythm during long, lazy hours together that first night, and his memory of their joining had haunted him with its beauty.

And yet, the subtle barrier of latex between them had veiled the beauty. He'd had no idea what he'd been missing...until now, when the veil was gone and the splendor of loving Charlie was dazzling him. He reveled in her liquid welcome. He treasured the inner caress she gave him each time he surged forward. With each thrust, she seemed to open even more deep inside, like some exotic tropical flower.

Her cheeks grew pink, her breathing quick and shallow. And oh, her eyes. He'd never seen them like this, luminescent and wide, as if she wanted him to see into her soul.

He wanted her to see into his. Then she would know how he cherished her. Right here, right now, he was dedicating his life to her in the only way he knew how. He was asking her to carry his child.

He felt her tighten around him, heard her breathing change. "Soon," he whispered.

Her response was breathless and urgent. "Yes, soon."

His pulse beat against his eardrums like heavy surf. "I'm going to come inside you, you fertile woman. And you're going to have our baby." He was dizzy with joy at the prospect.

"Yes." She arched upward. "*Yes.*"

Her convulsions brought on his. Her name rose to his lips as he pushed deep. With a groan of primitive satisfaction, he bestowed the most important gift of all—the future.

11

CHARLIE LAY TREMBLING beneath Mark as the power of their decision engulfed her. She could not doubt him now. They were joined forever.

"Ah, Charlie." He settled gently against her, the shirt he hadn't bothered to take off brushing her skin. He kept his weight on his forearms as he trailed lazy kisses over her eyes, her nose, her mouth. "My love," he murmured. "My life. Thank you for trusting me."

"I do trust you." And she wanted to be as close to him as she could get. Impatient with the barrier of clothes they'd been too frantic to remove, she slid a hand up his chest and began unbuttoning his shirt.

Mark lifted up so she could finish the job. When his shirt hung open, she snapped open the front clasp of her bra and pushed the lace cups aside.

He eased back down, nestling against her bare breasts. "Much better."

"Much." With a sigh she closed her eyes and allowed contentment to fill her. The visit from the DOAs had robbed her of that, but now she had it back. Birds twittered outside the tent and the creek babbled happily not far away. All was right with her world.

Mark resumed decorating her face and neck with kisses, and then he began to chuckle.

She opened her eyes. "What?"

"You lined up the tent so the rocks would be on my side, didn't you?"

After their spectacular lovemaking, she felt really guilty for all she'd put him through. He loved her so much, and she'd tortured him. "Was it awful?"

"Horrible." He nipped her earlobe. "But not nearly as bad as the bottle of water you dumped inside my sleeping bag. You must have been a terror as a little kid."

"I wasn't! I'm really not the type to pull mean tricks on people. It's just that—"

"I know." He ran his tongue along her jaw. "We all do crazy things when we're scared."

"I guess." Her heart beat a little faster. It was the perfect line to lead into his broken engagement history. Those other fiancées didn't bother her a bit, now, but she still would like him to tell her about them.

He gazed into her eyes, a smile curving his mouth. "But we are going to move the tent," he said.

"Okay." She waited expectantly. She would be so supportive and understanding that he wouldn't have to feel the least bit uncomfortable about all those past mistakes. Maybe she'd suggest that he take each of those women to lunch and apologize for what he'd put them through.

Or maybe not. She wasn't exactly jealous of those five beautiful women, but after all, he had been engaged to them, so he'd found them sexually attractive at some point. Instead of a lunch date, he could write them all letters. He'd become quite a good letter writer in the past three months.

His gaze darkened. "But maybe we won't move the tent right this minute."

"Okay." She was still sure that he planned to confess

everything and throw himself at her mercy. But then his kisses moved down below her collarbone, and she began to suspect he had other ideas. When he cradled her breast, she felt his penis stir and harden within her, and her body answered with a quiver of awareness.

"It's nice not to have to worry about condoms," he said in a husky voice as he rubbed his thumb over her breast. "I can stay inside you and start over whenever the urge takes us." He leaned down and kissed the tip of her breast. "I'll bet I can tease a few more climaxes out of you before we worry about moving the tent."

Her pulse raced in anticipation. "Maybe." Oh, well. Confessions could wait. They had more pressing matters. Six days ago he'd taught her how talented he was. He could almost talk her into an orgasm. Why deprive herself of his skillful attentions now?

"Did you know you're even sexier in a flannel shirt than in that red dress?" He caught her nipple between his teeth.

"No." The light pressure of his teeth sent a signal to her womb, coaxing her into that now-familiar spiral that would coil ever tighter until he touched the spring, sending her into ecstasy.

He released her nipple, leaving it damp. Then he blew softly over the super-sensitive tip. "You drove me crazy, all covered up in red plaid, your shirt tucked in so snug, your breasts pushing at the material, daring me to touch you."

"I...didn't mean to...drive you crazy." She was amazed how quickly he could make her breathless with desire.

"You did, anyway." He flicked his tongue back and forth, then blew gently once again. "And the buttons looked as if they would come unfastened so easily. I looked at you and my fingers shook because I wanted to undo those buttons so I could see these beautiful breasts. And you wouldn't let me."

She regretted every squandered moment.

"And I remembered how you tasted, Charlie." He stroked her breast, caressing her until she shivered. Then he eased her arms out of the sleeves of her shirt, so that she was finally naked. "I remembered how good it felt to take your nipple into my mouth, to roll it over my tongue, to suck on it until you were almost ready to come."

She moaned.

"Do you want me to do that again?"

"Yes, please, yes."

"Let's see if I can remember how you like it."

Oh, he remembered, all right. And he added a new dimension when he bunched the sleeping bag under her hips. With his mouth still at her breast, he began slowly thrusting, building the tension, propelling her beyond reason, beyond caring whether anyone could hear her cries of heavenly release.

This time he didn't follow her over the precipice. Releasing her breast, he shifted the angle of his thrust, taking it deeper to stimulate her in a whole new way. She quickly climaxed again, her body quaking with the impact.

While she was still gasping, he held her close and rolled to his back on his side of the tent.

"The rocks..." she said breathlessly.

"Ask me if I care."

"But—"

"Ride me, Charlie. Ride me and come again."

She was helpless to refuse him. She'd learned that once he coaxed her onto this roller-coaster, she became his willing slave. And so she braced her arms on his chest and moved her hips, gliding up and down, suffused with lusty enjoyment.

"I love watching your breasts jiggle when you move like that," he said in a hoarse, passion-filled voice.

She looked into his heavy-lidded eyes and a thrill of sensuality shot through her.

"I love watching that sweet bounce. And you feel so good. So very good." He clenched his jaw. "Slow down. Slo-o-ow down. That's it. Now hold still." He reached between her thighs and brushed his thumb against her pleasure point. "Come again," he whispered, his brown eyes dark with excitement.

She gulped for air and closed her eyes as his lazy caress brought her to the edge. Then he increased the pressure just enough to catapult her into another orgasm. She threw back her head and dug her fingers into his chest.

When her arms grew too weak to support her, he gathered her close and eased her over until they lay facing each other, still joined. She gazed at him in awe. No one had ever come close to pleasuring her as he could.

"I love you," he murmured. Then he cupped her bottom in both hands and looked deep into her eyes as he began a gentle rhythm. "I love you so much."

She could barely speak. "I...love you."

His strokes became faster and more powerful, the glow in his eyes more intense. "I'm a part of you, now. And you're a part of me."

"Yes." She gripped his shoulders and held on.

"*Forever.*" He thrust deep.

"Yes."

"Forever." He shuddered and closed his eyes.

She held him close and absorbed the pulsing rush of

his climax, her heart overflowing with love. She'd been a fool to ever doubt him.

AT LAST the moment had arrived, and Mark discovered he was more nervous than he'd expected. Charlie lay totally naked and relaxed on the soft flannel of her sleeping bag. She only needed one thing to make the picture complete.

But now that the time was here, he was worried that she might not like the ring he'd picked out. It didn't look like other engagement rings in the jeweler's case, but the first time he'd seen it he'd thought of Charlie.

He wanted it on her finger, tangible evidence of their bond, but in order to accomplish that he had to get past the moment of presenting it, the moment when she might indicate by some fleeting expression that the ring wasn't exactly what she'd had in mind.

With his other fiancées he'd allowed them to help him pick out the ring, because when it came right down to it, he hadn't known them well enough to make the choice without them. That in itself had been telling, although he hadn't understood the significance until now.

This time he'd wanted to pick out the ring by himself, and in the jewelry store he'd been so sure he'd found the perfect one. He realized that he'd attached a lot of importance to her reaction. If she didn't love it as much as he'd hoped, he would be crushed. He hadn't often allowed himself to be this vulnerable. Come to think of it, he never had.

Maybe he should get used to the feeling. Charlie had his heart in her hands, and she could do so much damage. She might not even know how much.

Well, now or never. Summoning what courage he could, he sat up and reached for his discarded jeans.

"Are you getting dressed?" she asked.

"No." He shoved his hand into the front pocket and his fingers closed around the black velvet pouch. "I...I wanted to...that is, I think it's time for me to—"

"Mark, don't be scared," she said gently. "I understand this could be nerve-wracking."

He glanced at her as he pulled the velvet pouch out of his pocket. She obviously knew what he was about to give her. Logic would tell her that he'd buy a ring this week. "You have no idea. Maybe we should have discussed it beforehand."

"Maybe. But I'm sure you had your reasons for not doing that."

"I did. I wanted to surprise you."

She looked puzzled. "Surprise me?"

He took the ring from the pouch. "Okay, it's not a big surprise. You've already figured it out." Holding the ring between his thumb and forefinger, he extended it toward her, his heart thundering with anxiety. He swallowed. "I hope you like it, Charlie. Because it comes with all my love."

Her eyes widened and she sat up. "A ring?"

He nodded. Maybe she was surprised, after all. He couldn't imagine what she'd been expecting, if not a ring. But he didn't have time to worry about that. He was too busy worrying about her reaction to his choice.

"A ring," she whispered, her gaze fixed on it as she took it carefully from him. "It's...oh, Mark." She glanced up, tears in her eyes. "It's two daisies twining together."

"Yeah." She either loved it or hated it, and he was in

agony wondering which it was. "I saw it and thought—"

"That I loved daisies," she said softly, staring at the ring as she slid it on her finger. "How perfect."

The breath whooshed out of him in relief. "Then you like it."

"I don't like it—"

He panicked.

"I *love* it!" She launched herself at him and threw her arms around his neck as tears rolled down her cheeks. "I love, love, love it. And I love you for knowing that I would love it."

"I didn't know for sure. I hoped." He was about ready to bawl, himself, out of sheer happiness that he'd guessed right.

She sniffed. "I need a really big hug right now."

"Me, too." As he gathered her into his lap, she wound her legs around his hips so they fit as neatly as two sections of a hinge. He wrapped his arms around her and held on tight.

Her voice was muffled against his neck. "Where did you find it?"

"I went to about five places." At last he could share what he'd been through this week. "And I kept looking at the ones that had just one diamond, and that didn't seem right for us. They even call them a solitaire. Did you know that?"

She nodded, her cheek rubbing against his shoulder. "Yes, I knew that."

"There's going to be nothing solitary about us," he said fiercely.

"Nope." She sounded so very happy.

Her joy filled all sorts of places that he hadn't known were empty. He was damned proud of himself for finding a ring that would make her cry. "So then I saw this ring, with two diamonds, each one in the center of a sweet little daisy. I think they call it filigree, or something like that."

"I call it gorgeous. I've never seen anything like it."

"That's the way it should be." He kissed her bare shoulder. "Because our love isn't like anybody else's, either."

"Nope." She sighed with obvious contentment as she rested her cheek against his shoulder.

Her curls felt like silk against his skin. He reached up and combed through them, loving the way they wound around his fingers. "When your hair starts turning gray, I don't think you should color it or anything."

She laughed. "Where did that come from?"

He continued to stroke her hair. "I don't know. I was just thinking about all the years ahead of us. We'll get gray, and maybe a little rickety, but—"

She leaned back to grin at him. "Rickety? Speak for yourself."

He basked in the happy light in her eyes as he grinned back. "Okay, so we won't get rickety. We'll be skipping over these hills when we're ninety-two. I only meant that I'm looking forward to all of it. I don't want to miss a thing, even the gray hair. It's all part of the deal."

Her eyes grew misty again. "Yeah, it is. We're going to have a great life, Mark."

"Show me how the ring looks."

Obediently she stuck her hand in front of his face, fingers spread.

He held it steady and surveyed the ring, now that it was on her finger. It looked even better than he'd imagined. "They have matching wedding bands that look like stems and leaves woven together. I have a picture in my backpack."

"I'm sure I'll love them, too."

"And it fits, right?"

"Perfectly." She turned her hand so she could admire the ring. "How did you do that?"

"Talked to Ashley."

"Really?" She gazed at him. "She sure did keep the secret well. I had no idea."

"I figured I could trust her not to tell." He'd enjoyed his conversation with Ashley on Monday. It had only confirmed what he believed—that she and Sam had something special going on. Sometime during the reception dinner he'd probably reveal the stories he'd made up about them. The good will of the wedding celebration and a couple of glasses of champagne would pave the way, and they'd be ready to laugh about the whole thing.

He'd been secretly relieved that Sam had been called out of town this weekend. If he'd stayed in Houston, he might have spent the weekend with Ashley and they'd have figured out the prank Mark had pulled. He wanted to confess before that happened. Less incriminating that way.

"So did you and Ashley talk about anything else?" Charlie asked.

He looked into her eyes. "You. She told me that you have a tender heart, and if I ever so much as bruise it, she'll run me down with her car."

Charlie nodded. "That sounds like Ashley."

"I told her she didn't have anything to worry about."

She met his gaze. "No," she said softly. "She doesn't."

CHARLIE HAD BROUGHT along her camping shower, a contraption that included a plastic bag to hold water and a shower curtain. She was glad they found a private spot to hang it, because Mark insisted on showering together, and the curtain didn't begin to hide their antics. The entire process took about two hours.

By the time they finally fixed a meal it was closer to dinner time than lunch, and Charlie, who'd had nothing to eat since the afternoon before, gobbled everything in sight. Then they moved the tent to a softer spot, built up the fire, and sat in low sand chairs in front of the flames as dusk settled over the campsite. They moved their chairs so the wooden arms were touching and held hands.

They talked about the wedding. She told him about the minister, a young guy who liked to tell jokes. And she described the flowers and the music she'd chosen for the organist to play. They marveled at how similar their taste in music was. He said he'd have chosen exactly the same numbers.

She couldn't remember ever being this happy in her life. Her existence was nearly perfect. Ninety-nine percent perfect. All she needed to be absolutely, positively sure about this relationship was for Mark to tell her about his other fiancées.

Maybe now, while they sat gazing into the embers of the dying fire, he would open up. She decided to give him a boost. "Are you sure you don't want to invite your mother to the wedding?" she asked. "I don't feel right leaving her out."

"We can invite her if you want," Mark said, surprising her.

"Really?" Charlie felt better already. "That's good. I'd like that. What's she like, your mom?"

"Complicated."

"What does she do for a living?"

"Teaches college chemistry, graduate level."

"Wow. That's interesting." Charlie didn't miss the clipped way Mark was answering her questions or the tense set of his jaw.

"I suppose," he said.

"Aren't you proud of her?"

"I guess, but I feel as if I hardly know her."

Charlie couldn't imagine such a thing. "But she's your *mother*."

"Yeah, but she was always kind of remote." He seemed to make a visible effort to relax and his voice gentled. "She's what you'd call an absentminded professor, Charlie. If she'd been born a man, nobody would think anything about her preoccupied state of mind and her devotion to her career, but because she's a woman and she happened to have a kid, everyone expected her to pay attention to the kid."

"Well, yeah."

He shrugged and gave her a lopsided smile. "I survived."

"You told me in your letters that your mom was divorced. She never remarried?"

"Nope. Never even came close." He stared into the fire and rubbed his thumb over hers. "I used to think her marriage to my dad was so awful that she didn't want to risk another one. So finally I worked up the courage to ask her, and she said it wasn't awful, just a waste of her time. I think she might be one of those people who never should have married in the first place. She loves having the house and her little basement lab all to herself. Even having me around was a bother."

She heard the pain in his voice and squeezed his hand. "I doubt that."

"Oh, I don't. But like I said, I survived. I spent a lot of time over at Sam's house."

"Bless Sam and his family."

"I do. All the time."

"Then we should invite them to the wedding."

He smiled at her. "The kids are all scattered except Sam, but I was going to ask you if we could invite Sam's parents. I know we're keeping it small, but they are like my family."

"I wouldn't have it any other way." Even though he'd confessed nothing about his five engagements, she was beginning to understand how they could have happened. He'd been desperate to find someone and establish the happy home he'd never had, the one he'd envied every time he went over to Sam's. And yet he knew what divorce could do to a kid, so each time he'd realized that his coming marriage might not be a happy one, he bailed rather than taking a chance on hurting a child of his the way he'd been hurt.

Thinking back on his letters, she remembered a wistful note running through some of them, usually the ones he'd written in response to her telling him something about her mother and father, or her sister. She'd thought that was natural coming from someone who had no siblings and had been raised by a single mom. But she hadn't understood the depths of his loneliness.

Oh, yes, the reason for his five engagements was becoming very clear. And so long as he didn't see the potential for divorce with her, then that string was about to come to an end.

He gripped her hand tighter. "Charlie."

She turned her head.

His gaze was filled with yearning. "Come to bed with me."

Warmth flooded through her as she realized how much he needed her, how much he would always need her. Everything was going to be fine.

12

THEIR NIGHT TOGETHER was so exciting that Charlie forgot to worry about Mark's past. All that mattered was the very sensuous present. Besides, they still had lots of time for a discussion before he went back to Houston.

He was spending Sunday night in her apartment so they could apply for the license first thing Monday morning. Then he planned to drive back to Houston immediately. They both had a full week ahead of them in order to clear the decks so they could relax on their honeymoon. Charlie had exchanged assignments with another tour guide and would take out a group Tuesday through Friday in order to have the next seven days free.

But they didn't have to go back to work quite yet, and Mark's excellent lovemaking had put her in an extremely mellow mood by the time they returned to her apartment late Sunday afternoon. Camping with him had been great, but she was looking forward to spending some time together on a comfy innerspring.

"When do you want to call your folks?" he asked as they put her camping gear away in the locked storage cubicle assigned to her apartment.

After his description of his own family life, or lack of it, she had no trouble understanding his eagerness. "We can call them now, if you're ready."

"I'm ready." He followed her up the steps to her second-floor apartment. "A little nervous, but ready."

"They're going to love you, so relax." She believed they would, so long as they didn't hear about the broken engagements right off the bat. She'd already decided that even when Mark finally admitted the sad truth about his background, she would hold onto the information for a while and not tell her mom and dad until after the wedding. No point in making them worry when there was no reason. And they would worry.

In fact, they were probably worrying now, she thought as she unlocked the door to her apartment. No matter how good an impression Mark made on the phone this afternoon, they'd still prefer to meet him before the wedding day. Charlie wished that were possible. She'd never intended to spring a husband on them like this, but marrying Mark next Saturday seemed like the exact right thing to do.

Because she was aware of Mark's nervousness, she decided to place the call to her parents as quickly as possible. After she and Mark had each grabbed a bottle of water from the refrigerator, she picked up her cordless phone and speed-dialed her parents' number.

Her father answered. "Hi, Button," he said, using his pet name for her.

She heard a basketball game in the background and pictured him in the den where he probably was watching the Bulls on TV. He'd be wearing his favorite Sunday outfit, gray sweats with holes in the knees and a soft blue sweater that matched his eyes.

"How'd you know it was me?" she asked.

He chuckled. "Caller I.D. Just put it in this weekend. We weren't going to bother, but then every damned time we called your Uncle Jack and Aunt Mary, they'd answer with *Hi, Hank and Sharon!* Your mother couldn't stand it, them having one up on us, so now we have it, too."

Charlie laughed. Her mother and her Aunt Mary's fifty-year-old case of sibling rivalry had developed into a family joke. She felt a pang of nostalgia for the old neighborhood in Arlington Heights where she'd grown up surrounded by aunts, uncles and cousins. But she and Ashley had agreed it had been good for them to try their wings somewhere else. And now Texas was in Charlie's blood.

"So what's this I hear about some guy sweeping you off your feet?" her father said.

Charlie glanced at Mark, who was circling her living room studying her framed photos from her backpacking and rafting experiences. "He's pretty special, Dad."

Mark turned and gave her a heart-melting smile. Then he crossed the living room and sat beside her on her futon sofa.

"He'd better be special," her father said. "I'm not walking my Button down the aisle and handing her over to some schmuck."

Charlie had a sudden panicky image of her father walking her down the aisle and Mark bolting out a side door. But of course that wouldn't happen. It *couldn't* happen. Too much was at stake now.

Besides, Mark didn't act like a man who had any intention of running. At this very moment he was gazing at her with complete adoration and rubbing his hand along her thigh while he waited for his turn on the phone.

"Mark's terrific," she said. "As a matter of fact, he's right here. He'd like to talk to you."

Her father chuckled. "Oh, sure he would. He's probably as excited about talking to me as I was when I had to face your mother's old man for the first time. But the sooner he gets it over with, the better. Put him on."

"Now, Dad, you're not gonna treat him like you used to treat my dates in high school, are you?"

"Whadya mean? I was very nice to those boys."

"You scared the hell out of them! All that talk about your bayonet skills in the Marines. Honestly. They thought if they weren't careful you'd use those skills on them!"

"Instilling a little healthy respect for the older generation never hurts."

"Dad, now don't you—"

"Oh, I'll be a pussycat, Button," her father said with another chuckle. "Give him the damned phone before he passes out from anxiety."

"Okay. Love you, Dad."

"Love you, too, Button."

As Charlie started to give the phone to Mark, she noticed a suspicious sheen to his eyes. She put her hand over the mouthpiece. "You okay?"

"Yeah." He cleared his throat. "It's just...the easy way you talk with him. The...the...love is so real."

Her heart squeezed and she leaned over and kissed him on the cheek. "And I'm going to share every bit of it." She put the phone in his hand.

He cleared his throat again and put the phone to his ear. "Mr. McPherson?" He paused. "Oh, okay, then. Hank. You know, it's a little late to be asking permission to marry your daughter, but—" He listened for a few seconds, and then he laughed. "Is that right? The ladder up to her window and everything?" He glanced at Charlie. "No, she didn't tell me about that. Yes, I definitely feel better now."

Charlie realized her father was describing how he and her mother had eloped thirty years ago, much to the dismay of both sets of parents. Come to think of it, her folks had set a precedent for this kind of hasty marriage. Maybe it would become a family tradition.

Mark laughed again and started talking about his adventures looking for the right engagement ring. She could tell from the light in his eyes that he was soaking up the fatherly attention and advice. She decided to leave the room and give him some privacy.

With a friendly pat on his thigh, she stood and walked out of the living room. She'd had that fatherly attention for twenty-seven years. She could afford to let Mark have it all to himself for twenty minutes.

Besides, she felt grubby and, fortunately, her apartment had a roomy bathtub. She stripped off her clothes as she headed for the bathroom and tossed them in a hamper once she reached it. Then she closed the door and started running water in the tub. Last of all she dumped in some of her favorite scented bubble bath.

A full-length mirror was bolted to the back of the bathroom door, and she paused for a minute in front of it. That was when it hit her—the woman reflected in that mirror could be pregnant.

Her heart beat faster as she laid a hand over her stomach. The concept was mind-boggling. And yet she hadn't been kidding Mark about the fertile women in her family. Both her mother and aunt had conceived their first children on their wedding night. Her uncle Jack, father of five kids, used to joke that all he had to do was hang his pants on the bedpost and Mary was pregnant.

Charlie was no expert on the subject of getting pregnant, but she was somewhere in the middle of her cycle, and she vaguely remembered that was a productive time of the month. If frequency of intercourse made any difference, then she and Mark had certainly covered that base.

Pregnant. The thought was a little scary, but mostly thrilling. Since the moment when Mark had suggested abandoning birth control, he hadn't backpedaled once. Far from it. He'd seemed absolutely determined that before the weekend was over she'd be absolutely, positively carrying his baby.

A man could cancel a wedding. He could cancel a reception and a honeymoon. But he couldn't cancel something like this. She smiled and turned away from the mirror. The DOAs were wrong. Mark meant business this time.

MARK FELT LIKE he'd known Hank for years when his future father-in-law turned the phone over to his wife, Sharon.

"Hello, Mark," she said, her voice warm.

"Hello, Mrs. McPher—"

"Nope, that won't do. Mrs. McPherson was my mother-in-law, and she was a dear lady, but she sucked her teeth while she sat and watched TV. You'd better just call me Sharon."

"Okay." Mark grinned. He could hardly wait to meet Charlie's parents. They sounded like a Midwestern version of Sam's.

"Charlie tells me you can cook," Sharon said, "which is a blessing, because she's not interested in the process unless you put her next to a campfire, and most modern kitchens aren't set up for that."

"I can cook." Mark continued to smile as he thought of Charlie's attempts to sabotage him with Saturday's breakfast.

"Well, I'm relieved." Sharon laughed. "The two of you won't starve. Now what about gifts? The relatives are driving me crazy up here because you're not registered anywhere. You'd better do something about that or you're liable to get about twenty-five very ugly cookie jars."

"I'm afraid we won't have time to register anywhere," Mark said. Then he had an inspiration. "Tell you what. How about if you ask them all to hold off, and we'll plan to come up there and visit over a long weekend. We'll get more organized about what we might need, and we can do the gift thing then."

"Oh, I would *love* that," Sharon said. "We can have a big barbecue in the back yard, and invite all the relatives...." She hesitated. "Unless you think a more formal reception would—"

"No!" Mark had already begun to envision the happy scene, and it was exactly what he'd longed for his entire life. "A barbecue would be great. Perfect. Tell us when you want us there."

"Over Memorial Day?"

"We'll do it. I'll make sure Charlie hasn't booked a trip, but if not, count on us."

"I'll do that." Sharon's voice quivered with excitement. "What fun." She took a deep breath and lowered her voice. "I realize you're getting married quickly, but Hank and I got married quickly, too. We were young and stupid, but it worked out, because we were desperately, hopelessly in love. I'm hoping you are, too. That's really all I need to know."

"We are."

"I can hear it in your voice. I can hardly wait until I can see it in your eyes. Then I'll rest easy."

"I understand," Mark said. "Don't worry. Charlie's my whole world."

"That's good. Very good. Listen, could I talk to her a minute? I want to consult with her about what I'm wearing. What's your mother wearing?"

Mark gulped. "Well, I'm not sure—"

"Oh, never mind. I wouldn't really expect you to know. Boys don't generally pay attention to those things."

"I'll get Charlie," Mark said, desperate to avoid the topic of his mother. He wondered if there was any way he could convince her to come this time. Obviously it would make a huge difference to Charlie, and probably to Charlie's parents.

He'd heard water running in the bathtub, so he carried the phone through the bedroom to the door and tapped on it while he kept his hand over the mouthpiece. "Charlie? Your mom wants to talk to you."

"Okay," she called through the door. "You can bring the phone in here."

He opened the door to a sight that made his tongue hang out—a rosy blond nymph in a bubble bath that almost, but not quite, covered her up. Instantly he began to develop an erection, which didn't seem quite kosher while he still had her mother on the phone.

She glanced at the bulge in his pants and grinned.

He felt himself blushing and he pressed his hand tighter over the phone's mouthpiece. "Charlie, it's your *mother*."

"I doubt if she'd be shocked."

"I know, but still."

"I won't splash, so she won't know where I was when

you brought me the phone." She stuck out a damp hand. "Would you dry me off?"

"Uh, okay." First he wrapped the cordless phone in one thick towel. Then he got another towel and dropped to one knee beside her to dry her hand.

All the while, clumps of bubbles kept shifting on the surface of the water. It reminded him of the view from an airplane flying through intermittent clouds, except here the landscape under the clouds was way more interesting. Instead of nubby, tree-dotted hills or the regimented pattern of a city, he was treated to a nipple peeking out here, a knee revealed there, and a heart-breakingly short glimpse of a triangle of gold curls darkened to bronze by the water.

By the time he handed Charlie the phone, he was a desperate man. His jeans pinched at the crotch as he gingerly rose to his feet.

"Hi, Mom!" she said, holding very still in the water. She kept her gaze fastened on Mark's fly and her grin widened. "Yeah, things are developing nicely here. Soon I'll have everything in hand."

He rolled his eyes to the ceiling. He needed to get out of there before she made him laugh...or strip down and climb in with her. Now there was an idea. But he'd wait until she ended the phone call. He'd spend the time in her bedroom, out of temptation's way. Slowly he backed out the door.

She waved a soapy hand at him.

Standing in her bedroom with the memory of her in the tub wasn't any easier on him, especially when he looked at the inviting expanse of her bed. On impulse he walked over and folded the sheets back. Then he closed the curtains over the room's only window and turned on a bedside lamp.

Just doing that made him get even more excited. The room wasn't as fancy as the Presidential Suite had been, but Charlie's touch was there, and that made it special. The comforter on the bed was hunter green, and over the bed she'd hung a print of a wolf peering through snow-covered branches.

The only other furniture in the room was a sturdy dresser that looked like an antique. The top was crowded with framed family pictures, but until he had Charlie to help him identify people, trying to figure out who everyone was made no sense.

Instead he started taking off his clothes as he listened to the murmur of Charlie's voice while she talked to her mother. Once again he became aware of the same easy affection she'd shown her father, and he experienced the same visceral reaction, the same deep yearning.

And then he had another insight. None of his other fiancées had been this close to their families. He hadn't thought that mattered, but maybe, on some level, it had mattered a great deal. Besides creating his own little family, he wanted to be part of an extended one, too.

God, he hoped Charlie was pregnant. He'd thought about it the whole time he was talking to her mother. Mentioning the possibility of grandchildren to her was a little premature. No, *very* premature. But he'd wanted to, anyway. He had a feeling that she'd be pretty damned excited about the prospect.

By Memorial Day they'd know if Charlie was pregnant. What a homecoming that could be for her. And for him. He couldn't pretend that he wouldn't think of it that way, as his homecoming, too. The visit might mean even more to him than it would to her.

Charlie's voice grew slightly louder. "Love you, too, Mom. See you soon. 'Bye."

Mark quickly finished undressing. With all the love-making they'd done so far, their chances that Charlie was pregnant were already good. But he wouldn't mind making them even better.

CHARLIE LAID THE PHONE beside the tub and was considering getting out when Mark walked through the door, naked and ready for action. The sight of his aroused body took her breath away. Knowing she'd caused him to become that way made her feel like a million bucks.

She gazed up at him and that lovely tension he inspired began coiling inside her again. "Maybe it's time I got out."

"Not necessarily." His gaze swept hungrily over her. "I was thinking of coming in."

"Really?" She tried to judge whether they'd both fit. It would be fun trying, at least. "Then I'll make room for you." She rose to her knees as he approached the tub.

As he stood next to her and started to get in, it struck her that she was missing a golden opportunity. She was in a perfect position to give him a thrill before he climbed in with her.

The woman she used to be wouldn't have been so bold as to suggest it. But because of the way she and Mark had started out, because he thought of her as bold and daring, she had become that person.

"Hold still a minute," she murmured.

"What—" He gasped as she curled her fingers around his penis.

She glanced up at him. "May I?"

His lips were parted, his eyes glazed over with passion. "Oh, babe, you never have to ask permission."

"I'll remember that." Her damp hands slid easily

over his hot, smooth shaft. She wasn't experienced in
this, but she was tuned in to him, and what she lacked
in knowledge she planned to make up for in imagination.

"I'll remind you." He drew his breath in sharply as
she dipped her hands in the water and stroked him
again.

When she twisted her hands lightly in opposite directions, he moaned with pleasure. Good. She was doing
something right. Teasing him even more with long, lazy
swipes of her tongue, she gripped and twisted gently
again.

"Oh, *Charlie.*"

"Like that?" Still caressing him, she gazed upward.

His gaze was hot and intense, and he seemed transfixed by the sight of her loving him this way. He buried
shaking fingers in her hair. "You know it."

"I thought so." Still keeping her gaze locked with his,
she took his penis slowly into her mouth.

He groaned and started to shake.

Man, she was loving this. What a feeling of power.
Looking up at him while she put him through such
sweet torture made it all the better. His eyes darkened,
then darkened even more. She continued using all her
weapons—hands, mouth and tongue. The more
aroused he became, the more she ached, but she was
having too much fun to be concerned about her own
satisfaction.

He began to pant, and his shaking grew worse. Finally he squeezed his eyes shut, gripped her scalp and
eased away.

"But don't you want more?" she murmured. She
knew he'd enjoyed every second of his little treat.

His laugh was a hoarse bark. Still cupping the back of

her head, he opened his eyes and sank to his knees on the bath mat. His gaze was hot and his fingers tightened on her scalp. "Yes," he whispered fiercely. "More, more and still more." Then he kissed her, plunging his tongue into her mouth.

She wrapped wet arms around his shoulders and hung on for dear life as his kiss grew more frenzied. Still devouring her mouth, he rose, drawing her up with him. Then he lifted her from the tub.

Instinctively she wound her legs around his hips and he carried her, dripping water and suds, to the bedroom. Her heart pounded in frantic rhythm with his. This was the kind of man she'd longed for, the kind who would lay her wet body on the bed without a thought about soaking the sheets, the kind who needed her so desperately that he couldn't wait for towels.

He had to be inside her, *now*. He thrust deep and kept thrusting until he rocketed them both into space.

13

DRIVING BACK to Charlie's apartment complex after taking care of the marriage license paperwork the next morning, Mark couldn't believe how much he was looking forward to saying the vows. He wished he could do it today. The idea of leaving Charlie and going back to Houston didn't seem right.

"Maybe I should just kidnap you and take you home with me," he said.

She sighed and squeezed his hand. "I'd be a willing captive, but it probably wouldn't be a good idea. I need to be here and you need to be there, at least until Saturday."

"That sucks." He brought her hand to his mouth and nibbled on her fingers. "By the way, do you have any bookings over Memorial Day weekend?"

"Not yet. I try to avoid it, because so many backpackers are out then that there can be gridlock on the trails. Why?"

"I sort of told your mom we'd come back there for a visit." He glanced her way to see if she minded.

Apparently not. She was grinning from ear to ear. "You did, huh?"

"She wanted to know what to do about the relatives buying presents, and I told her we'd had no time to register anywhere. I thought we could take care of that after the fact and then go up to Chicago for a party. Your mom seemed to like the idea."

"Oh, I'm sure she loved it." Charlie laughed. "I'll bet she's planning a barbecue in the back yard."

"She did mention something about that." Mark was thrilled that Charlie didn't have anything scheduled and they could plan the trip. When he got back to Houston he might start looking into the flights.

"I hope you're ready," Charlie said. "She'll invite every last one of the clan, and I have to warn you that some of them are crazy. They'll probably make you pitch horseshoes and play croquet until you drop. And the water-balloon fights usually get way out of hand."

Mark pictured the scene as he navigated the streets of Austin. She had no idea what such a prospect meant to him, but she would find out. "I'm gonna love it," he said softly.

"I hope so. And if you don't like Jell-O salad you're in trouble, because there will be at least six kinds."

"I'll eat every one." He stopped at a red light and looked at her. "By Memorial Day we should know."

"Know what?"

"If you're pregnant."

She flushed and looked almost shy. "Oh. I guess so." She looked at him from under her lashes. "If I'm not, it won't be for lack of trying."

"And I cherished every minute of it."

"Me, too."

As he accelerated away from the intersection, he gripped her hand tighter. "I want you to be pregnant. I want to be able to tell your folks, and your whole family, that we're having a baby."

"My mother will go nuts."

"I'll go nuts." He turned into her street and sighed. "I

sure don't want to go back to Houston today. I want our life together to begin right now."

"I wish it could. But Saturday isn't so far away. We'll—hey, that's Ashley's car parked in front of the apartment."

Mark wouldn't have known the sleek little Mustang belonged to Ashley because he'd never seen her car before. But as they pulled into the covered parking adjacent to Charlie's apartment building he could see that Ashley was sitting inside the Mustang.

"Shouldn't she be down at her shop?" For some reason finding Ashley waiting for them made him nervous. It wasn't part of the plan, and right now he didn't want a single glitch in the plan.

"The shop's closed on Mondays. But I still wonder what she's doing here." Charlie opened the car door and hopped out as soon as he turned off the engine.

Ashley got out of her car, too, and started toward them.

"Hey, you," Charlie called. "What's up?"

"Oh, I just thought I'd come and talk to Mark about something before he left for Houston," Ashley said. "I take it you two went to see about the license."

"Yes," Charlie said.

Ashley's glance flicked over her. "I thought you were getting sick on Friday."

"I—"

"She got over it." Mark came to stand beside Charlie and hoped his apprehension didn't show. "What did you want to talk to me about?"

Ashley took off her designer sunglasses and glanced up at him without the trace of a smile. "What's this I hear about a rash I'm supposed to have?"

Oh, shit.

"Rash?" Charlie asked. "What rash?"

Mark gazed at Ashley as his mind raced. "I guess you talked to Sam."

Ashley's cheeks grew pink, and for a second her indignant manner slipped. "Uh, yes, I did."

"And you probably told him about the transvestite thing." He couldn't believe the subject would come up during a telephone call, which might mean that she'd actually *seen* Sam this weekend, after all. That would explain the blush. But he was still in deep doo-doo.

Her indignation returned. "Yes, I did. And he's ready to kick your butt, or so he said. He's not happy with you, Mark."

Mark winced. He was definitely in for it, now.

"What's going on?" Charlie glanced from Ashley to Mark. "What's this all about?"

"Look," Mark said. "I can explain everything. I—"

"It seems that Sam's trauma with the transvestite was bogus," Ashley said, still gazing intently at Mark. "Not only that, but he told Sam that I needed rehabilitating, too. Supposedly I broke out in a rash every time I was attracted to a guy."

"*What?*" Charlie cried, turning toward Mark. "You made all that up?"

"Yeah, I did." He focused on Charlie. He cared about what Ashley thought, but Charlie was the one who concerned him the most. Should he spill the beans about the broken engagements now? Or did Ashley already know?

He'd guess not. Sam wouldn't take the liberty of telling, even when he'd found out the trick Mark had pulled.

"Why did you?" Charlie asked.

Damn it. The doubts were back in her eyes. This was

not the place to confess everything. She might cancel the wedding on the spot. If she did that, he would... well, he would have no more reason to live.

He took a deep breath. "Because Sam insisted on coming along. He thought I might move too fast, and he wanted to be there to slow me down. I felt sort of embarrassed that he insisted on being there for our first meeting, like I was some sort of sex maniac—"

"Are you?" Ashley asked.

"So I decided to work the whole thing into a double date," he finished, ignoring Ashley.

Charlie looked betrayed, and he hated that. He gripped her shoulders. "Dreaming up those stories was the only way I could think of to make Sam and Ashley go along with the date, because neither one of them needed a blind date, obviously."

"No, just a neurosis," Ashley said.

He continued to focus on Charlie. "I was going to tell them both at the reception, and I hoped we'd have a good laugh over it."

"Ha, ha." Ashley folded her arms over her chest.

"You should have at least told me this weekend," Charlie said.

"You're right. I should have. And I apologize for that. Charlie, I love you so damned much, and I'm petrified that something will come between us." He lowered his voice. "I beg you not to let this shake your confidence in me. It was a dumb thing for me to do, but at the time it seemed like the only way to make sure we had the best possible start."

She gazed into his eyes, and slowly her frown disappeared. "We did have a good start," she said.

"We sure did."

"A wing-ding of a start." A smile tugged at her

mouth. "I guess I can't be too hard on you, considering the rocky bed and the soggy sleeping bag and the burned breakfast. Oh, and the headache."

"Yeah," Ashley said. "What happened with that headache? I thought it was supposed to develop into something debilitating."

Mark vaguely realized that Ashley must have been in on the scheme of Charlie's fake illness, which meant she was the pot calling the kettle black, but he didn't even feel like making a point of it. He smiled back at Charlie as relief flooded through him. "As I said, she got over her headache."

"Seems like," Ashley said.

"So you forgive me?" he asked Charlie.

"Uh-huh."

"I believe I'm the one you should be asking for forgiveness," Ashley said. "And Sam."

Feeling generous, Mark turned to her. "I do ask it, Ashley. And I'll talk with Sam the minute I get back to Houston. For some reason I didn't think he was getting back from San Francisco until sometime today."

There was that blush again. "The, uh, business didn't take as long as he thought it would, so he caught an earlier flight."

Charlie stood next to Mark. She stood very close. He could feel support radiating from her.

She studied her sister. "When did he get back?"

"Yesterday, around noon."

"And he called you yesterday?" Charlie asked. "How come you didn't come over to confront Mark last night? You knew we'd be home."

Ashley's gaze shifted. "Well, actually Sam didn't call. He drove to Austin from the airport."

Charlie began to smile. "Hmm. Sam arrived in Austin yesterday afternoon, but you're just now getting over here to lecture Mark. Why the long delay?"

"Well, we—"

"Never mind." Charlie walked over and hugged her sister. "I know why. I'm thrilled for you. I think Sam's terrific."

Ashley looked as if she might be having trouble keeping her anger stoked up. "He is terrific," she agreed, "but Mark shouldn't have made up those stories."

"Think about it, Ashley," Charlie said. "Don't you realize that if Mark hadn't cooked up that whole deal, then you'd have had no excuse to go on the date last weekend? You wouldn't have met Sam until the wedding, and you certainly wouldn't have spent the night with him just now. So there."

If Mark had been head-over-heels in love before, he was Charlie's devoted slave now. Not only had she forgiven him for his crazy stunt, she'd stood up for him when her sister would have continued to toss blame his way. He slipped an arm around her waist and gave her a subtle squeeze to let her know how much he appreciated what she'd done.

Ashley gazed at her sister for a long time. Then she glanced at Mark, and back at Charlie. "You do look good together," she said, almost to herself.

"That's because we belong together," Mark said. "I think it might turn out to be true for you and Sam, too."

Ashley's body language softened even more as the stiffness went out of her spine. "It's possible." Then she straightened and shook her finger at Mark. "But so help me, you'd better do right by this sister of mine. That threat to run you over with my car stands. And as you can see, I have a fast car, with a strong bumper and big tires."

"I'll do right by her," Mark said.

"Yes, he will." Charlie gave him an adoring glance. "And you'd better get on the road, Mr. Right. Didn't you have an appointment you didn't want to miss?"

He checked his watch. Sure enough, he was out of time. He'd taken all his stuff out of her apartment before they'd driven downtown so that he could leave immediately after dropping her back at the apartment. But leaving Charlie was like cutting off an arm.

He decided to make it quick so it wouldn't hurt so much. "I'll see you on Saturday," he said. "I'll call tonight." Then he kissed her hard and climbed back in his car. All the way out of the parking area he kept looking in his rearview mirror to catch a glimpse of her standing there watching him leave. The next time he saw her, she would be wearing white.

CHARLIE WATCHED Mark's black Lexus until it disappeared around the corner. Saturday seemed like an eternity away. She didn't want to guide her group of backpackers tomorrow. She wanted to be with Mark. Going into her empty apartment would be dismal. Their breakfast dishes were still in the sink, and the towel he'd used would be hanging on the rack in the bathroom. It would be filled with his scent. She—

"So I'm guessing you had sex, after all."

She blinked and glanced over at Ashley. For a moment she'd forgotten Ashley was there. And what had she just asked? Oh, yes. She'd asked about sex.

"Yes," she said. *Unprotected sex.* She didn't plan to mention that to Ashley, who would go into orbit if she heard that.

"So I'm assuming he came clean about the broken engagements."

"Well, no, he didn't."

"He *didn't?* Oh, Charlie, that's not good."

"It doesn't matter," Charlie said. And it didn't. Not one bit. Mark had shown her in every way that counted that he expected to live the rest of his life with her.

"What do you mean, it doesn't matter?" Ashley jammed her sunglasses on top of her head, as if she needed both hands to make her point. "Of course it matters. His integrity is in question here. I just found out about that business with the rash and the transvestite. I was willing to let it go, considering how it all turned out, but you could be letting yourself in for a purple T-shirt, girl!"

"No, I'm not."

"How can you be so sure?"

Because he wants me to have his baby. But that was a private decision between her and Mark, and besides, Ashley might put a different interpretation on it. She might think Mark was irresponsible.

"I'm just sure, that's all," she told her sister.

Ashley let out a long, exasperated breath. "Why did you go to bed with him if he didn't confess?"

Charlie opened her mouth to explain how Mark's endearing willingness to suffer had melted her heart.

"That's okay. It doesn't take much imagination to figure it out. When they coined the phrase *bedroom eyes,* they were referring to Mark." She gazed at her sister. "So the wedding's on?"

"The wedding's on."

"Then we'd better get cracking. We have lots of details to tidy up if you're really and truly getting married on Saturday."

Charlie felt a jolt of excitement. For some reason it

hadn't seemed completely real to her until this moment. She was getting married!

ON MONDAY NIGHT Mark drove down the tree-lined street where he'd grown up. He passed the Cavanaughs' place where cheerful lights were on in several rooms as usual, and he wished he were stopping there, instead. But he didn't need to make a personal visit to convince Sam's parents to attend the wedding. One phone call had been enough.

His phone call to Sam's folks this afternoon had gone a lot smoother than the late lunch he'd had with Sam today. Sam had been boiling on a couple of counts. One was the transvestite story. But Mark had taken his cue from Charlie and convinced Sam that without the wild stories, Sam wouldn't have met Ashley. Eventually Sam's lawyer logic had come into play, and he'd grudgingly admitted that discovering Ashley was worth whatever Mark had put him through.

But on the second point—that Mark had neglected to confess his past misdeeds to Charlie—Sam wouldn't budge. He was totally put out with Mark about that. He thought Mark should drive to Austin tonight and lay it all out for her.

Mark had refused, and he still wasn't sure why Sam was sticking with the wedding plans after that flat refusal. Maybe it had to do with Mark's decision to visit his mother tonight and plead with her to attend the ceremony. Come to think of it, Sam had lightened up considerably after Mark had told him about that. Sam was the only person in the world who had an inkling of the desolate landscape that had been Mark's childhood, and he'd offered to go along tonight as moral support. But Mark needed to do this by himself.

He parked in the drive of the two-story house. In contrast to the lights blazing from the Cavanaughs', the O'Grady house was dark, except for a faint light coming from the window wells in the basement where his mother had her lab. Even the front porch light was off.

Walking up to that darkened doorway, he once again became the lonely little kid who'd forced himself to leave the warmth of the Cavanaughs' home each night and return here, because he had some pride, after all. The Cavanaughs were good people who'd tried to console him by saying that his mother was brilliant, that she might even win a Nobel Prize someday.

He would have settled for lights glowing in the windows, a welcome hug, even company in front of the television set. He'd prayed for the day when he'd be old enough to go to college, and he'd chosen dorm life over an apartment, just so he could surround himself with noise, people and light. Lots of light.

As he used his key to let himself in, he wondered if he'd be able to get her attention tonight. His record wasn't very good on that score. When he'd lived here as a kid, he'd often ended up going to bed without ever having the discussion he'd wanted. Sometimes, when the matter was urgent, he'd written a note and stuck it under the coffeepot in the kitchen. But he wouldn't do that tonight.

Once inside the door he pushed the buzzer she'd installed that sounded down in the lab, a device she'd created so she'd know whenever he'd arrived. He used to wonder if she even heard it. Flicking on lights as he went, he started down the steps to the basement.

He knocked on the door before opening it. Sure enough, she was sitting on a swivel stool with her back to him, hunched over several petri dishes. Her half glasses were perched on her nose, her laptop computer was positioned to her right and the fingers of her right hand rested on the keys.

Selena O'Grady was slim and still very pretty, with only touches of gray in her dark brown hair. He knew she'd never color it. She wouldn't want to take the time. She rarely even got it cut, leaving it long enough to catch up in one of those big butterfly clips at the back of her head.

As usual, she had on sweats and an oversized T-shirt, her at-home uniform. On campus she wore slacks, blouses and blazers, which might or might not go together, depending on whether she was in the middle of a big project. She was usually in the middle of a big project.

As he gazed at her absorbed in her work, his heart gave a funny little lurch, and he realized that the resentment he usually felt when in the presence of his mother was gone. She'd been a mere twenty-two when she'd had him, certainly not old enough to understand that she shouldn't have a kid, given her need for this work of hers.

She'd only followed what society had preached to all young women in those days. He wondered if his forgiveness had to do with his love for Charlie, and he decided it probably had everything to do with that.

He cleared his throat. "Hi, Mom."

"Hi, Mark." Her voice sounded typically distracted, and she didn't turn around. "Just give me a minute here."

Once those words would have made him angry. She'd said them a million times, and then she'd left him hanging, sometimes for hours.

Tonight he smiled. "I can't give you a minute, Mom.

I need all your attention, and I need it right now. It's a matter of life and death."

She spun around on the stool and pulled off her glasses. Her eyes were wide. "What did you say?"

Damn. He should have tried that line years ago. He walked toward her. "I'm getting married."

She rolled her eyes. "No, you're not, but I'm sorry to hear that another sweet young thing expects you to."

"No, this time I really *am* getting married, and I want—no, *we* want you to be there."

She fluttered her hand at him. "Like I said before, you can let me know after the fact—not that I really expect that to happen." She sighed. "I'm sure this is my fault, somehow. If you want to go into therapy, I'll pay for it."

He didn't contradict her. Some of his problems were her fault. But he couldn't blame her anymore, now that he realized that from the beginning she'd been doomed to fail at motherhood. If she'd known that beforehand, he wouldn't be here.

"I don't need therapy," he said. "But I do need you to come to this wedding. It's Saturday."

"Saturday? That's only—" She paused in confusion. "What day is this?"

"Monday." He couldn't help grinning. She was so flaky.

"Monday. Hmm. I thought it was Tuesday. Anyway, Saturday is only five days from now."

"Which is five too many for me. Mom, I want you to be at this wedding. It's in Austin, and you can ride down with—"

"Austin? You're not even getting married in Houston? Well, then it's out of the question. I can't spare the time from this project, even if I thought you would go through with it, which I'm afraid you won't. I wish you would finally marry someone, because you need a family. I know that. Let me pay for some therapy."

"No therapy. I'm going through with this wedding. And I want you there."

"Oh, Mark, I just can't. Now, if you'll excuse me, I need to get back to work." She swiveled the seat of her stool around until she was facing her petri dishes again.

A week ago he would have let it go at that. He crossed to where she was sitting, gripped her shoulders and turned her to face him.

She stared at him in astonishment. "Mark?"

He crouched down so that he could look directly into her eyes. "Listen to me, Mom. For all those years when you were too busy with your work to pay attention to me, I never begged you to give up your work because of something I needed. Never. I never thought I was important enough, or that what I wanted was important enough. Now it is."

"But—"

"I'm marrying Charlie on Saturday, and we're going to have a family soon. Before you know it, you'll be a grandmother. And if I have anything to say about it, you'll be a damn good one, because I'm going to be a real pest, starting now. I want you to plan on that wedding. Sam and I will pick you up at ten for the drive to Austin. And I won't take no for an answer. I love you, Mom, and I want you there on my special day."

She stared at him in shock for several long seconds. Finally she took a shaky breath. "Well, if you put it that way...."

"That's the way I'm putting it." He smiled at her. "So it's settled. Ten on Saturday. I'll call you at eight and remind you."

She nodded, looking dazed. "That's a good idea."

He gave her a quick hug and kissed her on the cheek. "I'll let you get back to your project, now."

"Okay."

He turned and walked toward the door leading upstairs. On impulse he glanced back, fully expecting her to be engrossed in her work again.

Instead she was gazing after him, a tiny smile on her face. "I'm happy for you, Mark," she said.

"Thanks, Mom." He took the stairs two at a time, and when he exited the house, he left every light he'd turned on still burning.

14

"I'M SURE HE'LL BE HERE any minute, Button."

"I'm sure he will, too, Dad." As Charlie sat in the recreation hall of the church twenty minutes after the wedding should have started, she fought to stay calm. But if one more person told her Mark would be there any minute, she might scream. Although her poor father meant to reassure her, his comment didn't help.

Everyone had tried to reassure her, even the five women who didn't believe Mark would ever show up and had driven down from Houston today to be with her in her hour of need. She wished they hadn't come.

First of all, she'd had to explain their presence to her parents. Although her mom and dad had tried to stay positive after she'd insisted Mark would not make her victim number six, his lateness was damning him with each minute that passed. Secondly, the DOA group's presence reminded Charlie that each of them had once been as confident as she that they would become Mark's wife. And they'd each suffered a huge disappointment.

But Mark would be here, and he would say his vows this afternoon. She had to believe that or go crazy. He was late, but he would be here.

The original rendezvous point had been Ashley's apartment. Charlie's parents were staying there, and so Charlie had decided to get dressed there, too. Sam,

Mark and his mother were to have arrived at Ashley's an hour before the wedding was scheduled to begin. Charlie was clinging to the knowledge that Mark had convinced his mother to attend the wedding. That had to be significant.

But they hadn't shown up thirty minutes past when they were due and there had been no answer at either Mark's or Sam's apartment when Charlie had called. Ashley had decided they should leave a note on the door and go to the church to meet the only other guests, Sam's parents. All the while Charlie had worked to stay calm.

The scheduled time for the wedding had come and gone while Charlie, Ashley and their mother and father had waited in a small room off the main sanctuary. Still no Mark. Then the DOAs arrived.

Finally they'd decided to abandon protocol when the minister suggested they all adjourn to the church's recreation hall. Charlie had given up on making a grand entrance in her dress and now sat, her veil thrown back and her shoes off while she tried to ignore the wall clock nearby. Everyone else struggled to keep a conversation going except Mark's ex-fiancée, Deborah, who made numerous calls on her cell phone trying to find someone who could locate Mark.

Watching her, Charlie wished Mark didn't hate cell phones so much. If he had one, he'd be able to call her from wherever he was. Or maybe he'd found a telephone and had left a message. She mentioned it to Ashley and they both ducked into the church secretary's office to call and check the messages on their answering machines. Nothing.

As they were leaving the small office, Charlie touched her sister's arm. "I hate saying this, don't even want to think it, but what if...what if there's been...an accident?"

Ashley's gaze was troubled. "I thought of that, too, but I didn't want to bring it up unless you did. The police wouldn't call either of us if that happened."

"They would call Sam's parents, though." Charlie put a hand to her churning stomach. "Maybe we should ask them to check their answering machine messages, too."

Ashley nodded. "Maybe we should."

So after that, three people trooped into the church secretary's office every few minutes.

Finally Charlie couldn't stand it any longer. She got up and faced the people sitting around on folding chairs. "I don't know what's happened," she said, "but this is getting more and more uncomfortable for me, and probably for everyone here. If it's all right with Ashley, I think we should all go back to her apartment and wait there. At least we can give people something to eat and drink." She glanced at Ashley. "Maybe something strong to drink."

Deb snapped her cell phone closed and stood. "The DOAs have that covered," she said. "We have plenty of booze stashed in the van in anticipation of this."

Her assumption that Mark would decide against the marriage filled Charlie with righteous anger. Feeding that anger was a growing fear that Deb might be right. She wasn't about to reveal that fear. "He *is* coming," she said. "I don't know what's happened, but he will be here."

Deb's gaze was filled with sympathy. "I hope so. I truly do."

"He will be here," Charlie repeated with as much

conviction as she could muster. But the doubts had started to creep in.

DRESSED IN HIS tux shirt and slacks, Mark paced the shoulder of the road getting dust on his shiny black shoes as he muttered every foul word in his vocabulary. If his mother hadn't been within earshot, he would have belted those words out and directed them right at Sam.

Damn it to hell, he *knew* they should have brought the Lexus. But Sam had been so all-fired hot to drive his baby over, arguing that he didn't much like Mark's Lexus and he'd have to drive it all the way back to Houston once he dropped Charlie and Mark off at the airport in the morning.

Sam finally got off his cell phone. "Road service should be here soon," he said. "They lost us on the system the first time I called, but now they promise to be here ASAP. In the meantime, we can sit here and admire the bluebonnets."

Mark had been happy about the bluebonnets two hours ago. He'd been thrilled that the wildflower show had begun in time for his wedding day. But at the moment he didn't care a damned bit about flowers. He gave the phone in Sam's hand a malevolent glance. "What kind of stupid cell phone only takes calls for road service, anyway?"

"It's the kind I like, okay? You don't even have one, period, so don't give me your crap. I don't want a regular cell phone for the same reason you don't. I don't want a leash. This one does exactly what a cell phone is supposed to. It works fine for road emergencies."

"Yeah, it works just dandy, except if someone loses us in the system, whatever the hell that means. And if we had my car, we wouldn't even *have* a road emergency," Mark added, glaring at his best man. "But no, we had to bring your pile of junk."

"Don't you talk that way about Betsy. If you hadn't made me stop the car to locate the dang wedding rings, she'd have taken us all the way to Austin."

"Yeah, and *then* the battery would have died in front of Ashley's apartment." Mark was furious, furious and scared. Things weren't going according to plan. "Why in God's name didn't you replace the battery this week?"

"Who replaces a battery before it dies?"

"In a critical situation like this, I would have! And about those rings, how could you not have them right in your pocket? Why were they packed in your suitcase in the trunk, for crying out loud?"

Sam threw up both hands. "It seemed logical! So shoot me."

"I just might. I can't imagine what Charlie must be thinking. It's a damn good thing I didn't tell her about those five other times I called off the wedding, which is what *you* wanted me to do, remember? If she knew about those, and we ended up being this late, she'd think I was backing out."

"Well, you're not," Sam said. Then he peered at Mark. "Are you?"

"Of course I'm not! How dare you say that?"

"I'll give you five good reasons."

"Oh, yeah? I have half a mind to leave you here and hitch my way to Austin!"

Sam stepped up nose-to-nose with him. "Well, what's stopping you, buddy-boy?"

"I am." Selena O'Grady walked over to the men and put both hands between them, pushing them firmly apart. "Honestly, you boys sound like you're eight years old and fighting over your blessed baseball cards. Yelling at each other isn't going to get us there any sooner."

Mark stared at her in amazement. He didn't think she'd ever heard one of his childhood arguments with Sam. He'd always assumed she was too preoccupied with her work.

As he looked down at the exasperated, totally parental expression she wore, a goofy grin tugged at his mouth. "You know what? You sound just like a mom," he said, without thinking. Oops. He watched in horror as her eyes filled with tears. He'd never seen that happen in twenty-nine years.

Her voice quivered. "I am a m-mom. I know I haven't been a very g-good one, but I've loved you the best I could."

His throat tightened. "I know you have. I didn't mean—"

"You're grown up now." Her lower lip trembled. "But I thought about what you s-said, that you'll make sure I'll be a good grandma." She sniffed. "You don't have to worry about that. I w-will b-be." And she began to cry.

Mark was scared to death that he'd start crying, too, right here in front of God and Sam and everybody. "Of course you will," he mumbled, and gathered his sobbing mother into his arms.

"Don't." She tried to squirm away from him. "I put on m-mascara. I'll get it on your shirt."

"I don't care." He cradled her head against his chest and his vision was a little blurry as he looked over at Sam, to see how Sam was taking this.

Sam swallowed, like he was having trouble keeping it together, too.

That made Mark feel a little better. In fact, he felt a lot better. Now it seemed like having the car break down was almost worth it. But he was still worried sick about what Charlie was going through. She could be thinking all sorts of horrible things. But at least she didn't know about those five ex-fiancées.

"Here comes the tow truck," Sam announced.

"Thank God," Mark said. "Now maybe we can get in touch with Charlie and tell her we're okay."

BACK AT ASHLEY'S, Charlie considered getting out of her wedding dress, but that would be admitting in front of the DOAs that she'd lost hope. So she kept it on, which meant she took up way too much of the space in the apartment. Nobody complained.

The liquor began to flow and was offered to Charlie several times. She'd refused for several reasons. First of all, she'd have to go to the bathroom, and that was a major job with the yards of material surrounding her. Second of all, she had only the barest hold on her emotions. One glass of wine and she'd lose it and start blubbering. She didn't want to blubber. Last, and most important, she could be pregnant, and alcohol wouldn't be good for the baby.

So she sat on a small stool with her dress spread around her. She figured she looked like Wedding Barbie, but instead of her daisy bouquet, which was chilling in Ashley's refrigerator, she cradled Ashley's cordless telephone. Every once in a while pain in her fingers would remind her she was gripping the phone way too tight and she'd relax her hold.

When the phone did actually ring, she came up off

the stool and nearly dropped it. It caught in the folds of her skirt and she grabbed it before it tumbled to the floor. Then she had the toughest time pushing the right button, because her hands were shaking so much.

When she finally pulled back her veil and put the phone to her ear, she realized the room was dead silent. "H-hello?"

"Charlie, it's Mark."

"Mark." The room started to sway and she sat down hard on the stool. "Are you okay?"

"I'm fine. I'm so sorry. I—"

"No accident?" Her ears buzzed and she was giddy with relief.

"No accident. Listen, I—" The phone crackled with static.

"Mark! I can't hear you!" She pressed the phone so hard to her ear that her head began to ache. More static fizzed in her ear.

"I—" The phone cut out, then in again. "—can't—reschedule—"

Her heart hammered under the tight bodice of her dress. "I can't hear you! Mark, what are you saying?"

Static was her only answer. Then the line went dead.

She took the phone from her ear and pushed the disconnect button while she prayed that he'd call right back.

Ashley was by her side, her voice tense. "What did he say?"

"I'm...I'm not sure. The reception was bad." Charlie was trembling, but she was determined not to lose it in front of all these people. "I'm hoping he'll call back."

Her mother put her arm around Charlie's shoulders. "You must have heard something, honey. Is he coming?"

Charlie had heard something, and the longer she held a phone that wasn't ringing, the more those words echoed in her head. *I'm so sorry. I can't reschedule.*

"Is everybody all right?" Sam's mother asked.

Charlie glanced up and noticed the woman was pale with worry. "Everybody's all right," she said, sounding like an automated message. "There was no accident." *I'm so sorry. I can't reschedule.*

"Do you think they're on their way, Button?" her father asked.

Charlie glanced around at ten anxious-looking faces. She knew what the DOAs were thinking. Sam's parents had watched Mark do this five times, too, so they'd probably come to a similar conclusion. Her parents and Ashley were still clinging to stray bits of hope, but she could tell the hope was fading fast.

Once she told them all what Mark had said, the hope would be gone. She only knew one thing at this moment. She couldn't bear to sit here and have everyone shower her with pity. Fortunately she'd hung the keys to her Miata on the rack Ashley kept by the front door.

She stood and handed Ashley the phone. "He's not coming," she said.

Everyone started crowding around her and talking at once.

"And I need to be alone!" she shouted above the din. For some reason she wasn't crying. Apparently she was too numb to cry.

The hubbub died down as everyone gazed at her as they might look at the victim of some horrible crime. Well, she was a victim, and she needed to come to terms with that and move on. She could do that best where she could hear the whisper of the wind through the trees and the gurgle of water over smooth stones.

She took a deep breath. "I need to be by myself for a while," she said. "I know that won't make you all real comfortable, but I promise to drive carefully."

"You're not driving," her father said. "That's out."

She leveled a look at him. "Yes, I am driving, Dad. I know I've made a dumb mistake in thinking Mark would marry me, but I'm not going to let that dumb mistake ruin my life. I need you—" She paused and turned to include everyone.

As her pulse raced, she stopped to take another breath before continuing. "I need all of you to demonstrate your confidence in me by letting me go off and think about this alone. I learned this a long time ago in the outdoor adventure business. If you treat me like a smart person who made a dumb mistake, I'll get over this. If you treat me like a dumb person who needs to be coddled and protected, I might not make it."

Her mother touched her arm. "Charlie, we only—"

"Please, Mom. Let me do this my way."

"Let her go," Ashley said.

Charlie turned to give her sister a look of gratitude. "Thanks, sis."

"Be careful," Ashley said.

"I will." Gathering her skirts, she walked to Ashley's front door, took down her keys and went outside with a rustle of white lace. She'd have to shoe-horn herself into the Miata, but she welcomed the challenge.

She welcomed any activity that would keep her mind busy and her thoughts at bay. The bluebonnets were in bloom. That was good. There would be plenty of traffic between Austin and her favorite campground. She'd have to drive carefully. Very, very carefully. And she would not cry until her tears could fall into the rushing creek and be carried away.

"I HATE CELL PHONES," Mark said as they barreled down the highway moments later. "Did I mention how much I hate cell phones? I hate the damned things. Hate 'em with a passion. When you don't need them, they work great. When you do, they don't work at all."

"How much did you get to tell her before the static took over?" Sam checked in the rearview mirror for cops and nudged the speedometer up a few more notches.

"I'm not sure how much she heard. She knows we're okay. Then I tried to tell her I couldn't get there for at least another thirty minutes. I asked if we could reschedule with the minister. I don't know if she heard any of it."

"We'll be there before you know it," Sam said. "Help me watch out for the black and white."

"Right. We can't get a speeding ticket, Sam. Make sure you don't get a ticket."

From the back seat, his mother reached forward and patted his shoulder. "It's going to work out," she said.

"Thanks, Mom. I hope so." He appreciated her comforting gesture, especially considering they'd been so rare in his lifetime. But he had a really bad feeling about this. A really bad feeling.

When they pulled up in front of Ashley's apartment, he looked for Charlie's little red Miata and couldn't find it. The bad feeling grew. Then he spotted Carrie's van. He knew it was her van—nobody else had that many bumper stickers in Latin.

His stomach began to churn. "I think the DOAs are here."

"Oh, Lord," Sam said.

"The what?" his mother asked.

"I'll explain later." He got out of the car. It was a miracle he remembered to help his mother out. He glanced at Sam. "I think I need to—"

"Go on," said Sam. "We'll follow at a more civilized pace, right, Mrs. O'Grady?"

Not waiting to hear his mother's reply, Mark took off at a sprint for Ashley's front door. By the time he rang the bell, he was puffing and his shirt was coming untucked from his slacks.

The door opened. Ashley grabbed him by the arm and dragged him forcefully into the room. "What do you have to say for yourself?"

He quickly surveyed the room and noticed every last person was standing and ready for action. If he'd ever wondered what a lynch mob looked like, he no longer had to. The Cavanaughs were there, and all his ex-fiancées, and he recognized Charlie's folks from the pictures he'd seen. But Charlie wasn't in the room. He prayed she was in another room. "Where is she?"

"We're not sure," Ashley said, her voice deadly calm.

His heart stumbled. "What do you mean?"

"When you called to say you weren't coming, she—"

"I didn't! I called to say we *were* coming, and to ask if we could reschedule the minister!" As panic set in, his gaze swept the room again, taking in all of his ex-fiancées. He knew the answer to the question, but he decided to make sure. "I take it she knows about the other times."

Deb nodded. "Yes, she knows."

He swallowed. "Okay, doesn't *anybody* know where she went? We have to find her."

Charlie's father stepped forward, his expression ferocious. "Son, are you saying you *do* want to marry my daughter?"

"More than anything in the world." He worked to

concentrate, despite the rushing sound in his ears. "We have to find her. Somebody must know where she went. What did she say when she left?"

"She said she had to be alone to think," Charlie's mother said. "When she was a little girl, that usually meant she wanted to go off into the woods somewhere."

And suddenly Mark knew exactly where Charlie was. "She's gone to the campground we went to last weekend."

Ashley nodded. "That sounds like what she'd do. She—" The doorbell interrupted her and her expression brightened. "Or maybe that's her!"

"That's Sam and my mother," Mark said.

"Oh," Ashley said. "Right." She went to answer the door.

Mark turned to the rest of the people gathered in the room. "Look, I'm going out there."

"So are we," said Charlie's father.

"Us, too," said Sam's mother.

"I think we got us a convoy," Sam commented from the doorway. "Where are we headed?"

Mark turned to him. "I'm sure Charlie's at the campground where we spent last weekend. Now that she knows about my past history, she thinks I've done it again. I have to go after her."

Deb stepped forward. "I have a brilliant idea. The DOAs will go fetch the minister and haul him to the campground, too. If you're finally willing to get hitched, then we plan to make sure it happens."

Mark gazed at her as his dream of a pretty little church wedding dissolved to be replaced by the image of marrying Charlie at the campground where they'd truly begun their marriage, where they might have conceived their first child. It felt right.

"I would appreciate that," he said. "I would appreciate that very much. If somebody will give me a piece of paper, I'll draw Deb a map so she can find the campground. Everybody else can follow Sam, my mother and me."

15

CHARLIE HAD THOUGHT she was perfectly rational when she'd headed out to the campground. But obviously she hadn't been operating on all cylinders, because she'd forgotten that by Saturday night on the first wildflower weekend in April the place would be packed to the gills.

She'd wanted to be alone, but that wasn't going to be easy. Every campsite was taken, and all of them were filled with *very* curious people. She had to admit she'd be curious, too, if a woman in an bedraggled bridal gown climbed out of a tiny car and started trudging over to the creek. She'd pulled off the veil about half-way through her journey and stuffed it under the seat, but she had no choice about the dress. It had to stay on.

Now she wished she'd changed clothes back at Ashley's when she'd had the chance. The DOAs had been right, of course, and only her stupid pride had prevented her from getting into something more comfortable. If she'd swallowed her pride and done that early on, she wouldn't be making a spectacle of herself in front of dozens of campers.

Braving it out, she picked her way through the trees, pausing every now and then to jerk her dress away from a bush where it had become entangled. Several times she heard the material rip, which gave her a certain amount of satisfaction.

Her goal was to cross the creek on a series of stepping stones and find some privacy on the opposite bank. Hiding herself while wearing a wedding dress with a skirt as big as the Liberty Bell would be tricky, but the trees grew closer together across the creek.

As she neared the edge of the water, two women about her mother's age approached. One was plump, the other fairly thin. Both had kindly faces.

"We don't mean to intrude," said the plump one, "but we wanted to make sure you...that you were okay."

"We both have daughters," said the thin lady. "And we...well, we wondered if you needed...anything."

Charlie looked over at the campsite where she guessed these two had come from and saw a couple of middle-aged men watching the proceedings. One was bald; one wore glasses. Probably the husbands. They reminded her of her dad.

She could see the concern in the expressions of the women, could even detect it in the stance of the two men. They acted so much like her parents would have under similar circumstances that something broke loose in her frozen heart. Her tenuous control snapped, and she sank to the mossy bank and began to sob.

She was vaguely aware of arms around her, comforting words, even tissues offered. Taking the tissues, she continued to cry. When the tissues she'd been given were soaked, someone thrust a cotton handkerchief toward her. The handkerchief reminded her of her father, who always carried one, and she cried even harder.

All her life she'd dreamed of a marriage as wonderful as her parents had. She'd believed that she'd have that with Mark. She'd been so wrong. And so very, very stupid. She never wanted to see him again, and yet...she could be carrying his child. Thinking of that, she soaked the cotton handkerchief, too. She began to wonder if she'd cry for the rest of her life.

And then, at last, the gusher slowed to a trickle, and finally she blew her nose and glanced up to find herself surrounded by sympathetic faces. The four original folks had been augmented by several more campers.

As much as she appreciated their humanity, this was exactly what she'd wanted to avoid. Her only consolation was that they didn't know just how much she'd been humiliated, or how completely she'd been warned beforehand.

She cleared her throat, but her voice was still husky with emotion. "Thank you all for wanting to help me," she said.

"Why don't you come over to our campsite?" said the plump woman. "We have some nice hot stew on the fire. We can make you some tea. I'll bet some tea would work wonders."

The kind offer threatened to start her off again. "Thanks, but if you don't mind, I'd like to cross over to the other side of the creek and have a little private time."

"But it's getting dark," said the husband with the glasses.

"We were afraid you were going to fall in." The other husband rubbed a hand over his smooth head.

From the way he said it, Charlie knew he thought she was planning to throw herself in. Drowning in this shallow creek would take some doing, but they probably didn't credit her with much common sense at this point.

She looked at all these well-meaning folks and knew she had to forge a compromise or they were liable to follow her across the creek. "As you've probably figured out, the groom didn't show up for the wedding."

Indignant murmurs sounded from the small crowd gathered around her.

"So I really need to go sit on my favorite rock across the creek and get myself together. I know I'll feel calmer if I can do that."

"Then take my flashlight," said the guy with glasses.

"That dress is the problem," said the thinner of the two women. "Let me give you something else to wear."

Charlie wasn't about to change clothes at this stage. But the woman was right—the dress was a problem. "Anyone have a knife on them?" she asked.

"For what?" The bald man stared at her suspiciously.

"I want to shorten this dress."

"Oh." He looked relieved and even loosened up enough to chuckle as he handed over his Swiss army knife. "Guess it's already ruined."

In more ways than one, she thought as she found the scissors attachment on the knife and started hacking about two feet off the hem of the dress. It was slow going, and finally the plump woman took over to do the back.

"There," Charlie said when it was finally done. She felt lighter already. Life still didn't look very rosy, but it wasn't as dark as when she'd arrived here. "If you'll throw that material away for me, I'll gladly take the loan of the flashlight, and I'll be back for a cup of tea in about an hour."

"Fair enough," said the husband with the glasses as he handed her the flashlight.

She ended up taking her shoes off and tossing them across the creek. Her good throwing arm guaranteed they made it to the other side. Then, using the flashlight to light up the stones that had become shrouded in darkness, she picked her way across the creek.

Despite being a little shaky, she made it with only one slip, and she recovered enough that she only got wet up to her ankles. When she stood on the far bank she waved the flashlight to let them know she was fine, and someone waved a flashlight from the other side.

Picking up her shoes and putting them on, she used the flashlight to find her favorite thinking rock, one she'd discovered the first year she'd moved to Austin. She settled on it with a deep sigh, closed her eyes and listened to the wind in the trees and the water lapping against the stones.

Yes, the sounds reminded her of Mark and the magical time they'd shared in this place. That was another reason for her to be here, sort of like climbing on a horse after you'd fallen off. She loved this little corner of the world, and she would not allow Mark to spoil it for her. She would not.

Hot tears pricked her eyelids and she blinked them back. Enough. She would waste no more tears on him. She gazed up through the trees and found a single star in the navy sky. And then she closed her eyes. For the first time in her life, she had no idea what to wish for.

As SAM DROVE them slowly through the campground, Mark spied Charlie's Miata. "Hot damn." His voice quivered with excitement. "She's here."

Sam pulled the Chevy up next to Charlie's car and turned off the engine. "She shouldn't be hard to spot."

"Nope. I shouldn't have a bit of trouble finding her." Mark hopped out of the car.

"I advise you to take this slow," Sam said.

"He's right," his mother added, climbing from the

back seat. "You've given her a real shock. Don't rush this and expect her to fall into your arms."

"Right." But motherly advice aside, Mark wasn't going to take it slow. He knew his Charlie. She wanted drama. If he had a chance in hell of pulling this off, he had to literally sweep her off her feet. But first he had to find her.

He approached the campsite nearest to Charlie's car. Four middle-aged people were sitting around the campfire. They all stood when he walked up.

"So you're the groom who didn't show," said one of the men, firelight glinting off his glasses.

"You ought to be ashamed of yourself," scolded a plump woman standing next to him. "That poor girl!"

"I feel terrible about it," Mark said. "And I'm here to make things right. Where is she?"

"I don't know if we should tell you," said the thinner of the two women. "Just exactly what are your intentions?"

"He's going to marry her," said Selena, stepping into the firelight. "And I should know. I'm his mother."

"And I'm the best man," Sam added, coming forward.

"And we're her parents," chimed in Hank McPherson, guiding his wife into the area with an arm around her waist. "We came all the way from Chicago to see this wedding, and by golly, we want to see it."

"Chicago?" asked the plump woman. "What part?"

"Arlington Heights," said Charlie's mother.

"*We're* from Arlington Heights, originally," the woman said, looking pleased. "What a small world."

It might be a small world, but Mark didn't see Charlie anywhere in it, and he was all out of patience. "Where is she?" he asked, wondering if she was hiding in the tent.

"Well, I guess we can tell him," said the guy with the glasses. "I mean, this looks like a wedding party. But you'd better plan on putting a ring on her finger, young man."

"We have the ring, right, Sam?"

"In my pocket," Sam said. "Just where you wanted it."

"And a minister is on the way," added Mark. "So where is she?"

"You're going to have the ceremony here?" asked the slim woman. "How exciting!"

"That's the plan, but we can't have it if you don't tell me where she is," Mark said, getting a little testy.

"She's gone across the creek," said the plump woman. "She said she needed to be alone to think, so we loaned her a flashlight and helped her cut a bunch off the hem of her dress so she could navigate the stepping stones."

"Oh, dear," said Charlie's mother. "I guess she won't be putting that dress in an heirloom box."

By the time she'd finished her sentence, Mark was halfway to the creek.

"Mark," Sam called after him. "It's dark out there! Take a flashlight!"

"Don't need it," he called back. "Charlie! I'm coming to get you, girl!" He stepped into the cold water, shiny shoes and all. Moonlight flickered on the water, but the stepping stones were only vague shadows in the darkness.

He didn't care. If he managed to find them, great. If he got wet up to his knees, he couldn't care less. In fact, if he fell in, that was fine, too. Only one thing mattered, and that was getting to Charlie.

Splashing through the water, he barely noticed the cold or how many times he slipped. And all the while he called to her and watched the woods. At last he saw her, a white, ghostly presence among the trees.

"You sure are making a racket," she said.

"That's because I love you." He lost his footing and plunged up to his knee in ice-cold water. He gasped and kept going. "And we're going to get married."

"I'll bet you tell that to all the girls."

He finally reached the opposite bank and grabbed a couple of roots to pull himself up and over. "I know you're furious because I didn't tell you, but I thought if I told you about the others, you'd doubt me." He walked toward her. "Now be honest, Charlie. If you'd known about those broken engagements, would you have been so willing to get married today?"

"I've known about them for a week and a half!" She hurled the information at him.

He felt sick to his stomach. "You did?"

"I knew when we went camping!"

As loud as she was getting, he figured the entire campground was listening. Sound carried in a place like this.

"I knew when we made love!" she bellowed. "Remember that? When you said we should make love without con—"

He leaped the rest of the distance and clapped a hand over her mouth. Then he grabbed her and held on tight.

She bit him.

"Ow!" He shook his hand, wondering if it was bleeding.

"That's only the beginning," she said, breathing hard

as she tried to get away from him. "I know how to fight, and I fight dirty."

"Don't fight me, Charlie." He struggled with her and was amazed at how much strength she had for a woman her size. All that backpacking had given her some muscles. "Marry me. Marry me now. The minister should be here any minute, and Sam has the rings, yours and mine. Come on, Charlie. Let's do it."

"I don't want to." She kept struggling. "I used to want to, but I don't anymore."

"Yes, you do."

"Nope."

"Okay. You leave me with no choice." He hoisted her, kicking and flailing, over his shoulder and started back toward the creek.

"Put me down or I'll scream!"

"You're already screaming." He winced as she landed some pretty decent blows on his back. "Now stop it, or we'll both go in the drink."

"It would serve you right!"

"Yeah, but you'll end up there right along with me." He started across, and he was none too steady with a hundred and ten pounds of furious female over his shoulder.

She kept on hollering. "I don't care!" she cried as she pummeled him some more.

"I do." He gasped for breath and wondered how John Wayne had done this in the old Westerns and made it look easy. "The ceremony will be a hell of a lot colder for both of us if we're soaking wet."

"There's not going to *be* a ceremony." She landed another hard blow to his shoulder blade.

It was enough to throw him off balance, and he knew

they were going down. He managed to pull her into his lap as he landed on his butt in the water.

"Oh!" She sat there in apparent shock as the water splashed over them.

He knew that he had to act while she was still dazed if he expected to win this one. Cradling her head with one hand, he kissed her for all he was worth. At first she wouldn't kiss him back.

But then—oh, thank God—then she did. And there they were, kissing like fools in the middle of the coldest water he'd ever had the misfortune to sit in. But he'd risk frostbite on his genitals if he could get the right answer out of her.

Between kisses he managed to ask the question, but his teeth were chattering. "Will you m-marry me?"

She lifted her lips from his for a moment, and her teeth were chattering, too. "Depends. Are you c-consumed with l-lust?"

"You b-bet."

"G-good. Then I'll m-marry you."

"But I also l-love you."

She kissed him quickly. "I know. I l-love you, too. Now let's g-get m-married before we freeze to d-death."

CHARLIE HAD ONCE attended a Jewish marriage ceremony in which the couple said their vows while wrapped together in a shawl. She and Mark weren't Jewish, but they were married wrapped in a blanket provided by one of the recently invited guests.

Their guest list had grown from a few people gathered in a picturesque church to a sizable group of campers crowded around the campfire in one of her favorite places in the world. Charlie decided it wasn't the wedding she'd dreamed of. It was better than that.

For purposes of warmth, the minister stood on one side of the fire pit while Charlie, Mark, Sam and Ashley huddled on the other side. At Deb's suggestion, the original members of the wedding—Mark's mother, along with Charlie's and Sam's parents and the DOAs—joined hands in a circle that enclosed the fire, the minister and the four participants. The host of campers, who had plenty of clothes to bundle up in, took their cue from Deb and formed another, bigger, circle beyond that.

Charlie was surrounded by love.

And as she looked into Mark's eyes and repeated the words of the age-old ceremony joining man and wife, she knew she always would be.

"You may kiss the bride," the minister said.

A whoop went up from the inner circle of guests.

"Hallelujah, sisters!" shouted Deb. "He finally did it!"

Mark smiled down at Charlie. "*We* did it," he murmured.

"I make you drool, right?"

"Absolutely." Then his lips claimed hers.

____Epilogue____

SPLAT! A water balloon broke in Mark's face. Sputtering and running, he hauled one out of his bucket and aimed it at Charlie's seventeen-year-old cousin, Zach. He missed.

"Guess they don't teach you to throw in Texas," Zach taunted.

"I'm softening you up for the kill," Mark called back.

"Naw, he's mine," said Suzanne, another cousin. She aimed a good one, but Zach dodged out of the way.

"I'm golden!" he said with a laugh.

"That's what you think." But just as Mark was ready to fire, Charlie started across the yard carrying a pitcher of lemonade.

Zach grabbed her and used her as a shield. "Hold your fire! I've got your girl."

Charlie grinned at Mark. "I'm nothing in the grand scheme of things. Waste him, Mark."

But he couldn't do it. Putting down his bucket, he held up both hands as he went toward her, smiling. "I give."

"Sucker," Zach teased.

"I sure am." He walked up to Charlie and winked. "Let me carry that."

Zach rolled his eyes. "Oh, here we go. You two are going to get sickening again."

Suzanne smacked the back of Zach's head. "Leave them alone. I think it's sweet."

"So sweet you want to puke," Zach said, but there was a twinkle in his eyes.

Charlie wouldn't give up the lemonade, so Mark kept her company over to the trestle table set up in a corner of the yard. He leaned closer. "When are we gonna tell them?"

"Right after everybody sits down," she said.

About that time, Hank, clad in an apron and shrouded with smoke from the barbecue, announced that the hamburgers and hot dogs were ready and people began lining up with plates and buns.

Mark looked at Charlie. "Which one of us is going to say it?"

Her face glowed with love. "You are."

He wanted to be the one, but he wasn't sure that was right. "It's your family."

"No, it's *our* family. And as its newest member, you should do the honors. It'll really put you in good with the relatives."

"Oh. Well, in that case, I'll tell them." Mark was so eager that he was guilty of rushing people through the line. And finally, after what seemed forever, the family, all twenty-six of them, were gathered around the long table.

When grace was over and Sharon started to pass the potato salad around, Mark stood and clinked his spoon against his lemonade glass. "Before we start, Charlie and I have an announcement to make."

She gazed up at him, her blue eyes sparkling.

He took a deep breath. "We've bought a house!"

Everybody clapped and cheered.

"Smart move, son," Hank said with an approving nod. "Interest rates are good right now."

Mark grinned. After all, it was his business to predict such things. "Yep. I know." Then he cleared his throat. "The house has a nursery in it," he added.

Eyes widened around the table, and then Sharon leaped to her feet and looked at her daughter. "Charlie?"

Mark squeezed Charlie's hand. "We're pregnant," he said. And in the ensuing round of congratulations, back-slapping and happy tears, he knew he'd come home at last.

Every mother wants to see her children marry
and have little ones of their own.

One mother decided to take matters into
her own hands....

Now three Texas-born brothers are about to discover
that mother knows best: A strong man *does* need a
good woman. And babies make a forever family!

Matters of the Heart

A Mother's Day collection of
three **brand-new** stories by

Pamela Morsi
Ann Major
Annette Broadrick

Available in April at your favorite retail outlets,
only from Silhouette Books!

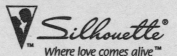

Where love comes alive™

Meet 50 loving dads in

babies

& BACHELORS USA

Take 4 FREE BOOKS,
Plus get a FREE GIFT!

Babies & Bachelors USA is a heartwarming new collection of reissued
novels featuring 50 sexy heroes from every state who experience the
ups and downs of fatherhood and find time for love all the same. All
of the books, hand-picked by our editors, are outstanding romances
by some of the world's bestselling authors, including Stella Bagwell,
Kristine Rolofson, Judith Arnold and Marie Ferrarella!

**Don't delay, order today! Call customer service at
1-800-873-8635.**

Or

Clip this page and mail it to The Reader Service:

In U.S.A.
P.O. Box 9049
Buffalo, NY
14269-9049

In CANADA
P.O. Box 616
Fort Erie, Ontario
L2A 5X3

YES! Please send me four FREE BOOKS and FREE GIFT along with the next four
novels on a 14-day free home preview. If I like the books and decide to keep them, I'll
pay just $15.96* U.S. or $18.00* CAN., and there's no charge for shipping and
handling. Otherwise, I'll keep the 4 FREE BOOKS and FREE GIFT and return the rest.
If I decide to continue, I'll receive six books each month—two of which are always
free—until I've received the entire collection. In other words, if I collect all 50 volumes,
I will have paid for 32 and received 18 absolutely free!

267 HCK 4534
467 HCK 4535

Name	(Please Print)	
Address		Apt. #
City	State/Prov.	Zip/Postal Code

* Terms and prices subject to change without notice.
  Sales Tax applicable in N.Y. Canadian residents will be charged applicable provincial taxes
  and GST. All orders are subject to approval.

DIRBAB01R   © 2000 Harlequin Enterprises Limited

Harlequin truly does
make any time special. . . .
This year we are celebrating
weddings in style!

A
Walk
Down
the Aisle

WEDDING CELEBRATION

To help us celebrate, we want you to tell us how wearing the Harlequin wedding gown will make your wedding day special. As the grand prize, Harlequin will offer one lucky bride the chance to **"Walk Down the Aisle" in the Harlequin wedding gown!**

There's more...

For her honeymoon, she and her groom will spend five nights at the **Hyatt Regency Maui.** As part of this five-night honeymoon at the hotel renowned for its romantic attractions, the couple will enjoy a candlelit dinner for two in Swan Court, a sunset sail on the hotel's catamaran, and duet spa treatments.

A HYATT RESORT AND SPA

Maui • Molokai • Lanai

To enter, please write, in, 250 words or less, how wearing the Harlequin wedding gown will make your wedding day special. The entry will be judged based on its emotionally compelling nature, its originality and creativity, and its sincerity. This contest is open to Canadian and U.S. residents only and to those who are 18 years of age and older. There is no purchase necessary to enter. Void where prohibited. See further contest rules attached. Please send your entry to:

Walk Down the Aisle Contest

In Canada	In U.S.A.
P.O. Box 637	P.O. Box 9076
Fort Erie, Ontario	3010 Walden Ave.
L2A 5X3	Buffalo, NY 14269-9076

You can also enter by visiting www.eHarlequin.com
Win the Harlequin wedding gown and the vacation of a lifetime!
The deadline for entries is October 1, 2001.

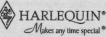

HARLEQUIN®
Makes any time special ®

PHWDACONT1

HARLEQUIN WALK DOWN THE AISLE TO MAUI CONTEST 1197
OFFICIAL RULES
NO PURCHASE NECESSARY TO ENTER

. To enter, follow directions published in the offer to which you are responding. Contest begins April 2, 2001, and ends on October 1, 2001. Method of entry may vary. Mailed entries must be postmarked by October 1, 2001, and received by October 8, 2001.

. Contest entry may be, at times, presented via the Internet, but will be restricted solely to residents of certain geographic areas that are disclosed on the Web site. To enter via the Internet, if permissible, access the Harlequin Web site (www.eHarlequin.com) and follow the directions displayed online. Online entries must be received by 11:59 p.m. E.S.T. on October 1, 2001.

In lieu of submitting an entry online, enter by mail by hand-printing (or typing) on an 8½" x 11" plain piece of paper, your name, address (including zip code), Contest number/name and in 250 words or fewer, why winning a Harlequin wedding dress would make your wedding day special. Mail via first-class mail to: Harlequin Walk Down the Aisle Contest 1197, (in the U.S.) P.O. Box 9076, 3010 Walden Avenue, Buffalo, NY 14269-9076, (in Canada) P.O. Box 637, Fort Erie, Ontario L2A 5X3, Canada.

Limit one entry per person, household address and e-mail address. Online and/or mailed entries received from persons residing in geographic areas in which Internet entry is not permissible will be disqualified.

. Contests will be judged by a panel of members of the Harlequin editorial, marketing and public relations staff based on the following criteria:

  - Originality and Creativity—50%
  - Emotionally Compelling—25%
  - Sincerity—25%

In the event of a tie, duplicate prizes will be awarded. Decisions of the judges are final.

. All entries become the property of Torstar Corp. and will not be returned. No responsibility is assumed for lost, late, illegible, incomplete, inaccurate, nondelivered or misdirected mail or misdirected e-mail, for technical, hardware or software failures of any kind, lost or unavailable network connections, or failed, incomplete, garbled or delayed computer transmission or any human error which may occur in the receipt or processing of the entries in this Contest.

Contest open only to residents of the U.S. (except Puerto Rico) and Canada, who are 18 years of age or older, and is void wherever prohibited by law; all applicable laws and regulations apply. Any litigation within the Province of Quebec respecting the conduct or organization of a publicity contest may be submitted to the Régie des alcools, des courses et des jeux for a ruling. Any litigation respecting the awarding of a prize may be submitted to the Régie des alcools, des courses et des jeux only for the purpose of helping the parties reach a settlement. Employees and immediate family members of Torstar Corp. and D. L. Blair, Inc., their affiliates, subsidiaries and all other agencies, entities and persons connected with the use, marketing or conduct of this Contest are not eligible to enter. Taxes on prizes are the sole responsibility of winners. Acceptance of any prize offered constitutes permission to use winner's name, photograph or other likeness for the purposes of advertising, trade and promotion on behalf of Torstar Corp., its affiliates and subsidiaries without further compensation to the winner, unless prohibited by law.

. Winners will be determined no later than November 15, 2001, and will be notified by mail. Winners will be required to sign and return an Affidavit of Eligibility form within 15 days after winner notification. Noncompliance within that time period may result in disqualification and an alternative winner may be selected. Winners of trip must execute a Release of Liability prior to ticketing and must possess required travel documents (e.g. passport, photo ID) where applicable. Trip must be completed by November 2002. No substitution of prize permitted by winner. Torstar Corp. and D. L. Blair, Inc., their parents, affiliates, and subsidiaries are not responsible for errors in printing or electronic presentation of Contest, entries and/or game pieces. In the event of printing or other errors which may result in unintended prize values or duplication of prizes, all affected game pieces or entries shall be null and void. If for any reason the Internet portion of the Contest is not capable of running as planned, including infection by computer virus, bugs, tampering, unauthorized intervention, fraud, technical failures, or any other causes beyond the control of Torstar Corp. which corrupt or affect the administration, secrecy, fairness, integrity or proper conduct of the Contest, Torstar Corp. reserves the right, at its sole discretion, to disqualify any individual who tampers with the entry process and to cancel, terminate, modify or suspend the Contest or the Internet portion thereof. In the event of a dispute regarding an online entry, the entry will be deemed submitted by the authorized holder of the e-mail account submitted at the time of entry. Authorized account holder is defined as the natural person who is assigned to an e-mail address by an Internet access provider, online service provider or other organization that is responsible for arranging e-mail address for the domain associated with the submitted e-mail address. **Purchase or acceptance of a product offer does not improve your chances of winning.**

. Prizes: (1) Grand Prize—A Harlequin wedding dress (approximate retail value: $3,500) and a 5-night/6-day honeymoon trip to Maui, HI, including round-trip air transportation provided by Maui Visitors Bureau from Los Angeles International Airport (winner is responsible for transportation to and from Los Angeles International Airport) and a Harlequin Romance Package, including hotel accomodations (double occupancy) at the Hyatt Regency Maui Resort and Spa, dinner for (2) two at Swan Court, a sunset sail on Kiele V and a spa treatment for the winner (approximate retail value: $4,000); (5) Five runner-up prizes of a $1000 gift certificate to selected retail outlets to be determined by Sponsor (retail value $1000 ea.). Prizes consist of only those items listed as part of the prize. Limit one prize per person. All prizes are valued in U.S. currency.

. For a list of winners (available after December 17, 2001) send a self-addressed, stamped envelope to: Harlequin Walk Down the Aisle Contest 1197 Winners, P.O. Box 4200 Blair, NE 68009-4200 or you may access the www.eHarlequin.com Web site through January 15, 2002.

Contest sponsored by Torstar Corp., P.O. Box 9042, Buffalo, NY 14269-9042, U.S.A.

PHWDACONT2

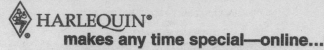
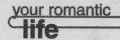